THE GIANT'S CAUSEWAY MURDERS

Private detectives step into troubled waters

ROBERT McCRACKEN

THE BOOK FOLKS

Published by The Book Folks

London, 2025

ISBN 978-1-80462-321-3

www.thebookfolks.com

*THE GIANT'S CAUSEWAY MURDERS is the
second standalone crime fiction title to feature Northern Irish
detectives Sidney and Ursula Valentine. Look out for the first,
THE MOURNE MOUNTAIN MURDERS.*

*Further details about it, as well as the author's other novels,
can be found at the back of this book.*

Dedicated to the memory of Dorothy Duncan, my greatest fan.

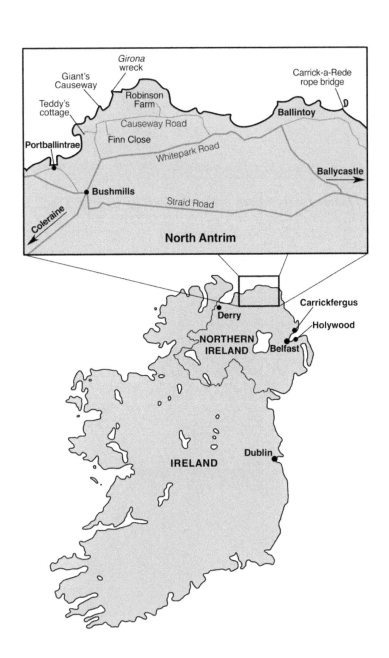

"Take great care lest you fall upon the island of Ireland, for fear of the harm that may befall you on that coast."

Don Alonso Perez de Guzman,
Commander of the Spanish Armada (1588)

Chapter 1

Teddy had been great, not the best catch in the world, but these days she couldn't afford to be choosy. Poor Teddy. He meant well. He'd enjoyed her company, her friendship, and the sex. She'd needed a fresh and exciting start. Teddy never asked awkward questions, and she never had to make up convenient lies. Her past life had been turbulent but didn't warrant discussion. She almost believed this relationship would last. Nine months, this time. It seemed a perfect match, but it was all too good to be true.

Poor Teddy. She dabbed her tears with the sleeve of her coat but couldn't still her trembling hands and the thumping of her heart. It felt as though at any moment it would burst from her chest. Her mind raced; her body shivered. But she had to pull herself together. It was the only way to survive. She was on her own again.

The whitewashed cottage had stood comfortably for generations amid green fields only a few yards from the rolling and tumbling waves of the Atlantic. Picturesque and yet somehow dangerous. Although she had a place of her own just a mile from here, Teddy's cottage had been the perfect love nest. But any dreams she had dared to indulge were shattered. All that remained now was for her to get out of this house, leave the area she'd called home, and flee the country.

She held open a large plastic bag that she'd found in a kitchen cupboard beneath the sink and began stuffing the clothes she kept at the cottage inside. Dashing to the bathroom, she swept her toiletries, make-up, and hairbrush into the same bag. She might have to dump all of it on her way to the airport. It didn't matter, so long as there was nothing left of her here. Nothing to indicate she had spent time in this house with Teddy. Finally, she wiped down the door handles and smooth surfaces in the bedroom and bathroom to remove her fingerprints. No point in making things easy for the cops.

Poor Teddy. She tried not to look at him on the carpeted floor, but she would have to step over him again to get downstairs. Strangely, he looked kind of happy lying there. Apart from the big, ornate knife in his chest. His lips had parted as if to smile, and even in death his waxed moustache looked immaculate. Teddy didn't get the evening he'd been expecting. A pity it all had to end this way.

She stepped over his booted feet, struggled down the narrow staircase with the plastic bag, and opened the front door. It was almost midnight. A chilly wind and pelting rain swept in from the sea, both invisible yet painfully striking her face. She heard the familiar distant rustle of waves striking the rocks, then for the last time turned and gazed back inside.

'Bye, Teddy, love,' she called between her sobs. 'I'm so sorry.'

She closed the door behind her and dashed to her car.

* * *

Ten minutes later, seriously spooked, she hurried into her own house. But she would never again feel safe, skulking at home, and there was no way she was ever going back to Teddy's cottage. It was far too risky, and she was a nervous wreck. Once the police found him, she knew, despite her efforts to remove all traces of herself from the cottage, that soon they would knock on her door.

It only took a few minutes. She booked a one-way flight online. Apart from travelling to Spain, she had no further plans. Maybe she could think of one on the way.

The suitcase she packed bulged from the poorly folded clothes stuffed inside. A pile of dresses and trousers lay discarded on the bed beside it. She pulled another case from the bottom of the slide-robe. But this wasn't intended to hold clothes. It was already packed; full of her life's history, a horrible one at that. And another unfortunate chapter had just been written. Running away from her problems had always been the easiest thing to do, and a dead lover certainly counted as a problem.

Still trembling with fear, she checked her watch and realised it was well past the time to leave. There was no time to even change out of her clothes. If she didn't make her flight, they would have her. And if they didn't get her, the police certainly would. Ash House prison was not how she pictured her future.

She closed the front door behind her, gripped the handles of the two cases and wheeled them down the drive to her car. She struggled to fit both into the boot and close the lid, but once done, she sat behind the wheel and took a deep breath. The street was quiet, just as it should be at this hour. She had a tearful glance at her house, gave a wistful smile and promised herself to shed no more tears. Her next life had already begun.

Suddenly, there was a tap on her window.

Chapter 2

It was a pity they were only paid by the hour. A fee for each hole could net them a fortune. Ursula Valentine took a picture with her phone then crouched to measure the diameter and depth of the pockmark on the asphalt road. Then she encircled it with a squirt of spray paint to make it easy for the contractors to locate and repair. It was tedious work for a woman with a low boredom threshold.

Her father, Sidney, sat in their van, entering the location of each pothole marked by Ursula into the Northern Ireland government database. Ursula knew the work of surveying potholes helped to pay the bills, but she craved excitement. Sidney, however, savoured peace and quiet. While she longed for the thrill of tracking down a rogue or unravelling a mystery, Sidney relished an afternoon on his recliner, a coffee, and custard-filled choux bun at his side, blues on the stereo and a decent book resting on his lap. Weather permitting, he could enjoy a pleasant view over the lough as ships came and went from the harbour and planes descended to Belfast City Airport. Today, however, it was pothole counting, and on Monday they had benefit fraudsters to pursue. Riveting stuff.

Only an hour since lunch, but Sidney would soon hint that it was coffee time. For some reason this afternoon, however, as Ursula examined another cavity in the road, Sidney appeared quite content to sit in their van. It was Ursula who needed a break. Kneeling by a rather large and water-filled gouge in the tarmac, she felt spits of rain on her face and decided that was her cue. She'd had enough. Stepping to the side of the road, she massaged her lower back, admiring her progress in the long residential street. Suddenly, she got a reminder of why it was a job that needed doing. A delivery van roared by, one of its wheels hitting her recently surveyed pothole and depositing a portion of the murky water within upon a hapless Ursula. The delivery driver, either unconcerned or perhaps oblivious to Ursula's drenching, carried on his way.

'Thanks very much,' she called, vowing never to use that particular supermarket delivery service in the future.

Her jeans and anorak were soaked. It made her decision to quit for the day an easier one. She tapped the van's passenger window and smiled with glee as her father jumped. He frowned as he lowered the window.

'Having a wee doze, are you?' she said with a smirk.

'Just resting my eyes,' Sidney replied, yawning.

'Aye, right. Does that mean you've had enough of this lark for today?'

In the strengthening shower, Ursula raised the hood of her anorak and waited for Sidney to make up his mind.

'How many have we done?' he asked.

'You tell me. Feels like hundreds. I'll be seeing potholes in my sleep. I suppose you already have, since you've been taking a nap.'

'I told you I was just resting my eyes.'

Ursula sat behind the wheel of the van and started the engine. If Sidney could call time on their work, then she would too.

'There's a pint of Guinness with my name on it at the Dirty Duck,' she said, driving off.

Sidney, a man intentionally slowing down into middle age, slightly overweight and with a small collection of ailments, including type 2 diabetes, high blood pressure and the odd bout of sciatica, didn't do much driving. It was a long story, but since they had begun their business venture, Sidney Valentine Solutions, he had suggested that Ursula take charge of transport. Ursula was happy to oblige; she didn't rate her father's skill on the road.

'If you're heading for the pub,' he said, 'you can get me something for my tea on the way home.'

'Calm your flaps, big man. I'm not going out until this evening. While you're snoozing this afternoon, I'll be making sure you've entered all the pothole info into the database correctly.'

'Of course I have.'

Ursula laughed heartily. 'I know what you're like.'

'Are you saying, albeit subtly, that you don't trust your old man's computer skills?'

'It's not so much about my trust, more about your competence.'

'That really hurts.'

Fifteen minutes later, they were back in Holywood. Ursula turned off the main carriageway between Belfast and Bangor into Kinnegar Road, drove past her local pub, the Dirty Duck, and thirty yards further on, stopped outside their apartment building. They lived on the second floor of a modern block of six apartments and had a commanding view over Belfast Lough. Ursula was first out of the van and darted across the road to escape what was now a downpour. Realising that Sidney hadn't followed, she glanced behind to see her father standing in the middle of the road. He was talking to a woman. Either Ursula proceeded indoors and began making the coffee, or she joined in the conversation. Sidney was right; she didn't trust him.

Chapter 3

Her name was Eve, and she lived in the Garden of Eden, a fact that had Ursula looking amused and puzzled. The woman, in her mid-thirties with a bob of chestnut hair, sat at their breakfast bar. She had a clear, yet pale complexion partially obscured by enormous dark-framed glasses that magnified her hazel eyes. Her blue jeans matched Ursula's in so far as they were soaked through. Ursula had taken the woman's coat and hung it over a door to dry. Sidney clocked the smirk on Ursula's face when the woman gave her name and stated where she lived. It did sound peculiar, but Sidney knew it was credible. He would explain it to his daughter later.

Ursula had prepared the coffee and set a plate of Hobnobs in front of Sidney and their visitor. Eve seemed grateful to be out of the rain. If Ursula hadn't intervened, they would still be outside in the middle of the road getting drenched. And she'd had to nudge her father when he stated that they weren't really private detectives, at least not the kind who took on the work the woman was suggesting. Ursula had steered them indoors. She wanted to hear the full story from the woman before she allowed Sidney to say no. Besides, once his interest was piqued, Ursula knew that he wouldn't be able to stop himself from sticking his nose in. He possessed a deep-rooted desire, arising from his wretched past, to strive for justice regardless of whether it provided financial reward.

Sidney cupped his coffee mug in both hands to get warm. His face was flushed.

'Have you told the police?' was his first question when Eve had recounted her story.

'I spoke to the police in Coleraine,' she replied. 'They said it was too early to be getting so worried.'

'How long has it been?' Ursula asked.

'I haven't heard from Fiona since Monday afternoon. I went to her house on Wednesday, but she wasn't there. Her neighbours told me that they hadn't seen her lately.'

'And today is Friday,' Sidney said. 'Has anything like this happened before with your sister?'

Eve looked intensely at Sidney as if admonishing him for asking such a question.

'No,' she said. 'But I really need you to find her, Mr Valentine.'

'We don't handle very many missing persons cases,' he said.

'Daddy!' Ursula glared at her father. 'Let's hear more of what Eve has to say first.'

'But?'

'Drink your coffee,' said Ursula. With Sidney put in his place, she addressed the woman with the biblical name. 'What do you think has happened, Eve?'

Removing her glasses, Eve wiped her eye with the sleeve of her jumper and sniffed. Ursula slid a box of tissues towards her.

'Thanks,' said Eve. 'There's not much to tell, really. It's so unlike Fiona not to call or text. We're very close. She wouldn't just go away without telling me. Something must have happened to her.'

'Was there anything strange going on?' said Ursula. 'Was she having any problems or worries, maybe with a husband or partner?'

Eve shook her head then blew her nose.

'Not that I know of. She's not married, and I don't think she was seeing anyone. Please find her for me. I can pay you, whatever it costs.' She lifted her D&G handbag from the table and opened it. Removing a plain brown envelope, she slid it towards Sidney. He peered inside then pulled out a wad of cash.

'Jeepers! There must be two grand here,' he said, leafing through the twenty-pound notes.

'There should be twenty-five hundred,' said Eve. 'Will it be enough to get started? I can pay whatever you want. It'll just take a couple of days to get more cash.'

Sidney looked at Ursula. Neither of them were used to this. He felt like Philip Marlowe in *The Big Sleep*. Usually, payments were handled by bank transfer and most came their way through various government agencies for their work on benefit fraudsters, accident claim investigations and, lately, for pothole surveys. Seldom did they have private clients, especially those who appeared to have loads of cash to chuck around.

Ursula knew why Sidney was looking concerned. Private clients always tended to mean big trouble. She cocked her head to the side and gave her father that big-eyed look, one that said 'please, Daddy' as if she were only fifteen and begging his permission to go clubbing with her pals. And, of course, Sidney was a complete sucker for her cute wee face.

He drew a deep breath then puffed it out.

'You know, Eve,' he said, 'people go missing for all sorts of reasons and more often than not, they turn up after a few days. Sometimes they just want to be alone for a while, clear their head, have a break.'

'Fiona wouldn't go off without telling me. We're very close.'

Sidney gazed from Eve to Ursula, then rubbed the stubble on his chin.

'We'll need to get some background on Fiona,' he said with a sigh.

'Oh, thank you so much.' Eve slipped from the stool and threw her arms around Sidney.

'I can't promise anything,' he warned.

'I know, Mr Valentine, but I really need your help.'

As soon as Sidney had relented and agreed to look for her sister, Eve pulled on her wet coat, preparing to leave. She removed a slip of paper from her pocket.

'That's her address,' she said, handing the note to Ursula. 'And I can give you my mobile number if you need to get in touch.'

'That's fine,' Sidney replied as Ursula copied Eve's number into her phone. 'But we're going to need a bit more information than her address. Can you give me a picture of Fiona? Where does she work? Anything about her neighbours? What are her interests? Can you think of any place she may have gone, if she just wanted to get away for a while?'

Eve looked thunderstruck at Sidney's requests but resumed her seat and began to fill in the blanks for her newly hired private detectives.

* * *

'Where do we start?' Ursula asked when Eve had finally departed. She joined Sidney by their picture window as he watched the ensuing rush hour of domestic flights on their approach to the airport.

Sidney began searching for a number on his phone.

'Well, I don't believe our new acquaintance has gone anywhere near the police,' he said. 'I don't think she would have come to us so quickly if she had. There's something she hasn't told us. Somehow, she also managed to avoid providing a photo of her sister or telling us what she looks like. All we have is a name and address and that Fiona works as a tour guide at the Giant's Causeway.'

Ursula listened while Sidney enquired of the police in Coleraine about whether a woman had been reported missing.

'You have no record of that name?' he asked. He winced at Ursula. 'OK, thank you. There's probably been a misunderstanding.'

He ended the call and looked with a sigh at his daughter.

'The police have no details of a missing woman reported by Eve McCabe. I knew we shouldn't have taken this on.'

'C'mon, Daddy, where's the harm?'

Chapter 4

Suppressing his annoyance at being duped by Eve McCabe, Sidney wasn't prepared to wait until Monday to begin his investigation. On Saturday morning, straight after breakfast, he and Ursula were on the M2, heading north.

Ursula felt the familiar tingle that a fresh adventure always brought. There might be danger ahead, but it was more appealing than a survey of potholes on the roads of Belfast.

'So, the Garden of Eden is a kosher address then?' she asked.

'Aye, it is surely. Garden of Eden is a wee cul-de-sac in Eden village, just outside Carrickfergus.'

'I'd never heard of it. I thought Eve was having a laugh, especially when she told us her name. I wonder if there's an Adam.'

'There is something going on with her, though,' said Sidney. 'She lied to us about reporting her missing sister to the police. I wonder why she did that.'

'Soon find out, won't we?' said Ursula with a chortle. 'Sure, we deserve a wee day out. It's been ages since we've been to the north coast.'

Sadly, the Ulster weather couldn't live up to her mood. The rain of the previous few days was on repeat as Ursula drove beyond Ballymoney then towards Ballybogey before making a right turn for the whiskey town of Bushmills. She had entered Fiona's postcode into the satnav on her phone. Finn Close was a small cul-de-sac of homes outside the town and less than a mile from the Giant's Causeway, Northern Ireland's most famous tourist attraction.

'This place looks more like a development of holiday lets than private housing,' Sidney commented as they turned off the main road and proceeded down a short lane.

Bordered by a mixed hedgerow of bramble and privet, the lane opened into a semi-circle containing six modern, detached bungalows resplendent in whitewash, blue slate roofs and block-paved driveways. The small development was surrounded by expansive green fields and patches of rough pasture. Several farms perched on the surrounding gentle hilltops were blessed with majestic views of the Atlantic Ocean to the north.

'It had been initially,' Ursula replied. 'I read about it online. The story even made the local news. They were built prior to Covid as holiday accommodation, but the builder panicked and sold them off when he thought he wouldn't recoup his money during the pandemic.'

Ursula stopped their van outside house number two, the address that Eve had provided for her sister Fiona.

'Right, off you go,' said Sidney.

'Me?'

'You were the one who wanted to do this. Go and see if anyone's at home. There's no car on the drive but check the house anyway.'

'Gee, thanks.'

Ursula got out of the van while Sidney looked on. Rain pelted down, and she pulled her hood up and scurried along the short driveway to the bright-yellow front door of the house. Each property in the close, it appeared, had a brightly painted front door in a different colour. There was no bell, so she used the sturdy brass knocker. As expected, she got no reply. Stepping to the left, Ursula cupped her hands on the window and peered inside. The compact lounge was dim, but she could make out a suite of furniture, a coffee table and a wall-mounted television. Two vases with flowers sat on a black-ash mantelpiece. Ursula guessed they were artificial or, if not, then quite recent fresh blooms. A pair of pink fluffy slippers lay by an armchair. Nothing seemed out of place in the room. There were no signs that someone had made a hasty exit and nothing to suggest that more than one person occupied the space.

To the right of the front door, Ursula gazed into what appeared to be the master bedroom of the cottage. The double bed was made, with a maroon duvet and matching pillows neatly arranged upon it. The wardrobes were closed, but the door to the hallway was ajar.

Ursula turned towards Sidney in the van and shrugged. He responded with a gesture intimating that she should look around the back.

It was a similar story. The back door was locked and, looking into the kitchen and dining space, Ursula saw nothing out of place. One last window afforded a view of the second bedroom, seemingly unused as such containing several large cardboard boxes and a small desk.

Padding back to the van, Ursula noticed several cars dotted around the close. It was Saturday, and probably a likely time to find people at home.

'Nothing,' she said to Sidney, slipping into her seat.

'Did you try the neighbours?'

'Hold on, give me a minute. Besides, it must be your turn to knock on a few doors.'

'Do you mean you'd have your old da traipsing about in the rain? I could end up with pleurisy, you know.'

'I don't even know what that is,' Ursula replied with a snort. 'But I can't bear listening to your moaning now, never mind if you were to catch a trivial illness.'

She climbed out of the van, applying more force than necessary to close the door behind her. Sidney winced at the noise.

There wasn't a car parked at house number one, so Ursula headed for number three where a well-worn silver Nissan hatchback sat on the drive. The front door was bright red, didn't have a bell but had a knocker like the one at Fiona's house. Ursula gave it a hefty tap and stood back, gazing around the close. It seemed a pleasant area in which to live, she thought, close to the coast, the Giant's Causeway and other tourist attractions. The pleasant, small town of Bushmills was just a kick along the road. It took a second bout of knocking on the door before it finally opened slightly to reveal a weary-looking man within. He wasn't forthcoming in greeting his caller. Ursula, head beneath her hood, beamed a smile at the peeved face of a man who looked like he had been disturbed from his sleep. The tatty pyjamas and bare feet were the real giveaway.

'Hello, sorry to disturb you,' Ursula chirped. 'I was trying to get Fiona next door, but she doesn't seem to be in. Any idea when she'll be back?'

'No.'

The door closed.

'Oh right, thanks for your time.'

She gestured with a shrug to her father as she marched down the drive and made for house number four where a racing-green Mini matched the colour of the front door. She rang a doorbell several times but got no reply. She quickly moved on to number five where a black Kia SUV was parked outside. This time, Ursula's knock gained an immediate response when a small elderly woman with short silver hair and a weathered face opened her orange door wide and beamed a smile.

'Hello there,' said Ursula, smiling back.

'Hello, dear. Only I'm not interested in anything you'd be selling, and I'm not a follower of one of those funny religions.'

Ursula chuckled. 'Sorry, it's nothing like that. I was just wondering if you can help me. Would you happen to know anything about Fiona at number two? I've been trying to get in touch with her on behalf of her sister. She's very worried about her. You don't know where she might have gone?'

The woman stared blankly for a second. Ursula wondered if she had understood the question, but then the woman turned around and shouted into the house.

'Bertie! Put the kettle on, we have visitors.'

'Right! Right!' came a gruff reply.

Ursula glanced towards their van.

'Do you want to bring your husband in with you, love?'

'He's my dad, but he'll be fine out there,' Ursula said with an impish smile.

'Well, come on in,' said the woman. 'Wipe your feet.'

Ursula was shown into a bright kitchen fitted with pine units and invited to sit at a round table in the centre. A sturdy-looking gent – Bertie, she assumed – grunted a hello as he poured hot water into a teapot. Ursula took in her surroundings. A large dresser against one wall displayed blue china serving plates and a model of an old sailing ship. The bottom shelf held a collection of books. There were a few well-known cookery volumes, some romance paperbacks and several textbooks about the Antrim coast, farming and ships.

'I didn't catch your name, love,' the woman said as she edged her husband out of the way and took over the preparation of the tea.

'Ursula Valentine.'

'And you're a friend of Fiona's?'

'No, a friend of her sister Eve. We were coming up this way and she asked us to check on Fiona. She hasn't heard from her for the last few days. She told me that it wasn't like Fiona not to phone her.'

'Bertie, will you go and sit down,' the woman snapped. 'You're getting in my way as usual.'

Bertie, in navy dungarees and leather slippers, tut-tutted then trundled over to the table and sat down. Ursula smiled and Bertie smiled back, rolling his lively eyes towards his wife. The man had a large head and wispy grey hair. His smile was friendly but, with several front teeth missing, a little off-putting. Ursula wondered when either of them was going to comment on Fiona. The woman, who had yet to introduce herself, eventually set three cups and saucers on the table and a large plate of buttered fruit scones. She checked the strength of the tea by pouring some down the sink then came to the table and filled the cups. She removed a carton of milk from the fridge and, without asking, added some to each cup.

'To tell you the truth, Ursula,' she said at last, offering the scones to her visitor, 'we don't know where Fiona is.'

'Oh,' said Ursula, 'I thought she might have mentioned something perhaps, if she was going away.'

Ursula appreciated the hospitality, but she was confused. Why go to this trouble, serving tea and scones, if the pair of them had no information to share?

'Nope,' said Bertie. 'Isn't that right, Cissy?'

Ursula stared from one to the other.

'Do you know of any reason why she might have gone away? Was it on business or maybe a personal problem?'

The big man smirked, and his shoulders jiggled as he chuckled.

'Oh, boyso, I can guess the reason she's taken off all right,' he said, his north Antrim accent strong and jolly.

'Bertie Robinson! What did I tell you?'

Ursula was suddenly a bystander in a domestic. She resorted to eating a scone. It was fresh and delicious. The tea was hot and strong.

'The wee girl only asked a question, Cissy,' Bertie hit back.

Ursula tried again.

'Has something happened to Fiona?'

Cissy frowned at her husband. It seemed the wife was having trouble sharing, while Bertie was finding the subject quite amusing.

'Done a bunk,' he said, seemingly unconcerned about further reprimands from Cissy.

'Any idea why?' Ursula asked.

'Money,' Cissy replied, looking angry. 'She's gone and taken all the money.'

Chapter 5

Sidney was well into a doze when Ursula got back to the van.

'Did you think I'd got lost?' she said.

'Thought you'd moved in,' he replied, yawning.

'They were a lovely couple; made me tea and scones.'

'And you didn't happen to think of your poor da languishing out here in the cold?'

'That's what you get for sending me to do all the work. Besides, you could have put the heater on.'

'Are you going to tell me what you found out?'

'Not that much, really.'

'No? But you took three quarters of an hour. What did you talk about?'

Ursula started the engine as Sidney waited for her to explain.

'Well, this Fiona woman has definitely scarpered. And it seems she's taken a load of money with her.'

'Where? Why? When?' Sidney barked.

'Don't know. Don't know. Last Tuesday, to answer your questions.'

'Is that it?'

'My new friends Bertie and Cissy confirmed that Fiona had gone, but they weren't prepared to give more details other than to say that she'd taken the money with her, whatever that means. They don't want to get involved in any trouble, but they gave me the address of someone who might know more and would perhaps be willing to help.'

Three minutes' drive took them back onto Causeway Road and heading towards Bushmills. A hundred yards further on, they turned right, entering a stony lane that led to an old, whitewashed cottage with a slate roof and a lean-to shed. Coming to a halt in the drive that melded with a rough garden and open fields beyond, they could see the National Trust car park in the distance, providing access to the coastal paths around the Giant's Causeway. A battered-looking red Vauxhall sat on a patch of grass a few yards from the two-storey cottage.

Ursula was grateful for the lull in the rain as they got out of the van. Sidney was keener to make a house call this time, hopeful for hospitality like Ursula had enjoyed at Bertie and Cissy's. She smiled at his eagerness, realising that her father would soon be looking for his lunch.

'So, this guy works with Fiona?' he asked.

'Yep. According to Cissy, they are freelance tour guides at the Causeway.'

Sidney knocked on the wooden door with his fist.

'There's a car here, so hopefully he's at home,' said Ursula.

There was no reply to Sidney's knock. Ursula moved to a quarter-paned window and peered inside.

'See anything?' Sidney asked.

'Nothing much.'

He gave the door another hefty rap with his fist. There was a click, and with a creak, the door swung inwards.

'It must have been on the latch,' Sidney said. 'Hello? Anybody home?'

There was no answer. The pair looked at each other doubtfully.

'What do we do?' said Ursula.

'He may have just gone for a walk. People in these parts don't always lock their doors.'

'Really? Is that still a thing? We're not exactly miles off the beaten track where strangers fear to tread. The main road to Bushmills is only a hundred yards away.'

'All right, smarty pants,' Sidney snapped. 'What do we do?'

'We'll give it ten minutes. If nobody shows up, we'll have a peep inside.'

Ursula wandered into an open field, trying to get a better signal on her phone, while Sidney ventured to the rear of the cottage. There was little to the place, just the house surrounded by a gravel drive, and the shed, open on one side and holding a stack of turf and logs. To the left, and detached from the cottage, stood an old byre which in more recent times seemed to serve as a garage or workshop. Sidney edged its battered wooden door open and gazed into the gloom. A sturdy bench sat to one side, with tools scattered around. On the earthen floor stood a petrol lawnmower and a rusty bicycle.

'Boo!'

Sidney jumped then turned to see his daughter with a naughty grin on her face.

'You trying to kill your old man?'

'Are we going to have a look inside now?'

Sidney stepped into the daylight.

'I'm not sure what I'd be looking for, Ursula. This man, you say, is just Fiona's work colleague. Unless he can tell us something in person, we're not likely to find much by snooping around in his house.'

'I suppose you're right,' said Ursula, 'but the door *is* lying open. It's not like we're breaking and entering. We can have a quick look and be on our way to lunch.'

Sidney stepped inside first. The downstairs smelled strongly of burnt peat, although the air felt cold. A room to the left of the step-in hallway was a throwback to at least the nineteenth century, with an inglenook fireplace, a heavyset table, rickety wooden chairs and a white Belfast sink below the window. A cramped staircase with an awkward turn rose over a low doorway. Ursula eased the door open and stepped inside a surprisingly comfortable lounge with a Persian-style rug on the stone floor. A dated, tiled fireplace sat below a large oil painting of an old sailing ship being tossed in a raging sea. But most of the wall space was taken up with bookcases. The volumes, both modern and quite dated, seemed to be mostly history or travel texts but also included complete sets of Conan Doyle and Dickens. There were more recent-looking books on famous naval battles, a biography of Elizabeth I and a ragged tome on Francis Drake. A pile of magazines lay on a bottom shelf, and among them Ursula noticed dog-eared copies of *Playboy* and *Penthouse*. Before leaving the room, she stole a peek through the brass telescope, resting on a tripod, and gazed from the window over the fields to the cliffs at the coast. She couldn't see much other than the white tops on the sea. Then Sidney called her.

He'd ventured upstairs, immediately regretting ever having entered the house and, more importantly, ever agreeing to search for Fiona McCabe. Ursula joined him on the cramped landing.

'What the…?' Her exclamation died as she cupped a hand to her mouth.

'He's been dead for a while, I'd guess,' Sidney said, matter-of-factly.

Chapter 6

Sidney and Ursula had been instructed by a uniformed police constable to remain by their van. They were told that a detective would be along shortly to interview them. Meanwhile, a fleet of marked police and forensic vehicles were taking up all the space in the lane and overflowing on the fields surrounding the cottage. Officers eyed them suspiciously as they came and went from the house. Ursula wondered how many of them had already decided that they were responsible for the murder. Sidney had taken to saying nothing at all, and Ursula reckoned he'd be getting grumpy soon. No lunch and now being at the centre of a murder inquiry was not what they'd envisaged for their day trip to the north coast.

When they'd had an eyeful of the bloodied corpse lying on the floor between the bedroom and landing, Sidney had immediately called the police in Coleraine, eleven miles away. Their search for the elusive Fiona had only just begun and already had become a lot more complicated.

A woman in black trousers and anorak strode from the house, gazed towards them, barked some orders at a young guy heading inside, then bounded their way. Ursula didn't think she looked happy. Maybe their discovery of a corpse had interfered with her Saturday afternoon.

She managed to smile weakly at Sidney and ignore Ursula. Funny how one single expression can say so much. It was peeved, impatient, pseudo-polite, suspicious and sarcastic.

'Any ideas on why the victim is dressed as a pirate?' she asked.

Sidney didn't do rudeness. This detective should have begun by introducing herself.

'And you are?' he asked.

Ursula saw the woman physically baulk at Sidney's question. She clearly wasn't impressed by Ursula's smirk either. After a brief pause, she rebooted the conversation.

'I'm Detective Inspector Pamela Kelso. And your names?'

Sidney and Ursula introduced themselves, and this allowed the detective to return to the subject in hand.

'Do you know the victim?' she asked.

'I think his name is Teddy,' said Ursula with a shrug. 'According to Cissy.'

'I didn't ask you his name; I asked if you were acquainted with him,' the cop said tersely.

'I think he is a tour guide at the Causeway,' Ursula added, feeling admonished. 'That's all we know.'

'What were you doing here?' Kelso asked. She looked sternly at Sidney.

Since she was being ignored again, Ursula allowed her father to field the question.

'We were looking for someone – thought she might be here,' Sidney replied.

'She?' said Kelso.

'Yep,' Sidney replied.

The detective glared at him, but Sidney was never going to say more than he had to. For him, the literal truth with a little suppression usually sufficed.

'Her name please,' Kelso persisted.

'Fiona,' Sidney replied.

'Surname?'

'McCabe.'

'And why did you expect to find this Fiona McCabe here?'

'She's a work colleague of Teddy's. She wasn't at home, and we'd driven all the way from Holywood to see her. I thought Teddy might know where to find her.'

DI Kelso did not appear convinced by Sidney's reasons for being at the home of a pirate who'd apparently been murdered. She changed tack.

'Did you touch or move anything inside the house?'

Sidney shook his head. 'We wouldn't even have gone inside if the door hadn't been lying open.'

Kelso wrote down their names and asked for ID.

'Don't go anywhere,' she said. 'I haven't finished with you.'

She marched off into the adjacent field and began talking on her mobile.

Ursula nudged her father. 'I think she has a wee fancy of you, Daddy.'

'You might be thirty years old, daughter, but I can still ground you for even suggesting such a thing.'

'So, what are you thinking about the pirate with the big fancy knife in his chest?' she asked. 'It's not like we're in the Caribbean.'

'I can't help thinking it has something to do with the elusive Fiona. I'm just sorry I ever let you talk me into taking this case.'

'I'm so hurt, but I know you don't really mean that.' Ursula pulled out her phone and started browsing, keeping one eye on the acerbic detective standing in a field.

Suddenly, with neither one noticing her approach, the cop stood before them once again. Her rather plain face, with pale blue-grey eyes and mousey hair, was still capable, it seemed, of looking even more irritated. But it was the controlled anger that most impressed Ursula.

'Right, you pair,' she said. 'Is that your van?'

'It is indeed,' Sidney replied sounding quite proud.

'I've just been checking you out. Call yourselves private detectives, eh? I suggest you get in your vehicle and head home. If I see either of you around here again, I will arrest you as suspects in this murder. Is that understood? If I need to get hold of you, I know where to find you. So, off you go.'

'Ach, thanks very much, Inspector,' Ursula said with a sickly smile.

The detective had already walked away and was heading towards the cottage. She turned her head. 'It's Detective Inspector.'

Ursula negotiated their van back along the lane, taking care to avoid the police vehicles lining the route.

'What now?' she asked her father.

'Well, I know you don't intend doing what she said. So, how's about some lunch?'

'Funny you should say that. I've just booked us into a nice wee hotel in Bushmills. And later, we can go back to Finn Close and try to find out what's been going on.'

Chapter 7

Sidney had always enjoyed visiting Bushmills. As a teenager with his mates, he'd fished for salmon in the River Bush that flowed through the town before it meandered to the ocean at Portballintrae. If pushed, however, he would admit that his adult regard for the area was down to the presence of the whiskey distillery. For Sidney there was no finer example of Ulster life than a good yarn with friends sat around a roaring fire on a cold night and a few wee measures of Black Bush to warm the cockles of your heart.

Over lunch at the Armada Hotel, a small, family-run establishment nestled within a row of terraced buildings in Main Street, Sidney phoned Eve to report on their dubious progress in tracing her sister. He asked her if she knew of

Fiona's colleague Teddy, but she said that her sister had only mentioned his name occasionally. Eve claimed to know nothing about money being a reason for Fiona to have disappeared.

Sidney required a little coaxing from Ursula to abandon a comfy fireside chair in the hotel lounge to revisit the folk at Finn Close. They began with a second attempt at Fiona's home at number two. As expected, there was no reply to Ursula's knock. As she ambled down the drive, she watched a sporty Volkswagen with alloy wheels, lowered suspension and custom paint job, thunder into the close and pull up in the driveway of house number one. The passenger door swung open, and Ursula was treated to booming music that her father would certainly not appreciate. He was apt to quote George Harrison in this regard – that rap music was spelt with a silent *c*.

A young woman in her late teens or early twenties, with blonde hair in a ponytail, jumped from the car and stomped to the front door of the house. She barged inside, slamming the blue door behind her. Ursula looked on as the music ceased, and a man of similar age to the woman emerged from the car, closed his door and dutifully locked it with his key fob. He gazed proudly at the gleaming motor, wiped a speck of something from the wing then, hands in the pockets of his jogging trousers, swaggered to the house. Before he made it inside, Ursula pounced.

'Excuse me!'

Ursula trotted up the drive and stood before the youth. He looked unimpressed at being collared. He had fine features but could have benefited from a little smile management. His eyes were scolding, and definitely not friendly.

'I've been trying to contact Fiona, next door to you. Any idea where I could find her?'

'Aren't we all, sweetheart,' he replied, his eyes instantly fixed on Ursula's ample bosom, a feature which frequently provoked such a reaction in certain men. Ursula was well used to it and on occasion had employed it to her advantage.

'Who's asking?' he said.

'I'm a friend of Fiona's sister. She hasn't heard from her for a while. She's a bit worried.'

The man grinned. As with DI Kelso, the expression carried all kinds of signals, none of which seemed friendly or sympathetic.

'Wouldn't mind a word with Eve myself,' he said. 'Bitch won't pick up on my calls. Pair of them are in it together, I reckon.'

'In what?'

The front door of the house opened to reveal the young woman. Ursula saw tears in her blue eyes, but she seemed eager to learn who was talking to her companion.

'What's going on? Who's she, Curtis?'

'Hiya,' Ursula tried, but the young woman was clearly in the middle of an issue with Curtis. She looked straight through Ursula towards him. Judging by the girl's manner, Ursula reckoned she could discount a brother–sister relationship.

'Is this her? Is this the tramp you've been screwing behind my back?'

'Wise up, Julie,' Curtis pleaded. 'How many times do I have to tell you, there is nobody else.'

Ursula cleared her throat. Loudly.

'Excuse me, folks,' she said, 'I'm really sorry to butt in. I'm just looking for Fiona. Curtis, you said something about Fiona and Eve being in it together. What did you mean?'

The couple exchanged uncomfortable glances. Then Julie, aside from having just referred to her as a tramp, now addressed Ursula for the first time.

'Who are you?'

'I'm Ursula, a friend of Eve's. I'm trying to find Fiona.'

'Curtis, get rid of her, will you? I'm getting one of my migraines; I can't deal with this hassle right now.'

Julie slammed the front door again, leaving Ursula to face a simmering Curtis.

'Any chance you could answer my question?' she asked.

'If I were you, I'd just clear off. And if you see Eve, you can tell her this isn't over. Not by a long way.'

He pushed past her and went into the house.

Ursula noticed that something had fallen from the man's pocket when he'd stormed off. She stooped and picked up a small plastic bag containing a white powder.

Sidney, watching from the van, was eager to hear news. He lowered his window as Ursula approached.

'Well, anything?'

'I'm beginning to think they're all a bit loopy round here. Must be the fresh sea air. And yer man dropped his stash.' She waved the bag then walked on by, and with little expectation of success, pressed the doorbell of number four. The green Mini was still in the driveway.

'Let's hope I get a normal human being this time,' she mumbled to herself.

Looking towards the van, she chuckled as she watched Sidney get out and stroll to the only other house they had yet to visit. She pressed the bell again, but her attention was now firmly upon her father and the woman he was chatting to on the doorstep of number six. In a flash, it seemed, Sidney had disappeared inside, leaving Ursula, without success at the green door, to wander back to their empty van.

At that point, Bertie emerged from number five and padded to his car.

'Hey, Bertie,' Ursula called. 'Who lives at number four?'

'Aye, that'd be young Natalie,' he replied.

'Young Natalie?'

'Aye.'

'I don't suppose you know if she's at home? Her car's in the drive.'

'Aye, so it is.' The man climbed into his SUV without another word.

'Well, thanks anyway, Bertie.' She watched as Bertie drove away then returned to wondering how Sidney was getting on. With the way the day had gone so far at Finn Close, she imagined having to break into number six to rescue her father from a mad spinster who'd tied him to a radiator and was force-feeding him fruit scones.

Chapter 8

Sidney regarded Eleanor Martinez as quite pleasant if a tad reserved. But she had readily invited a complete stranger into her tidy home and willingly engaged in conversation. She was, however, the kind of woman who had a knack of wheedling the truth from an unwary soul, particularly a man like Sidney. For some inexplicable reason, he found himself revealing exactly who and what he was before he got any information from her. But she seemed impressed.

'I didn't realise there were such people as private detectives in our wee corner of the world,' she said. 'It sounds very American.'

Eleanor had perched herself on the arm of a chair looking down upon Sidney who'd all but disappeared in her deep cushioned sofa. She was a woman in her late thirties, with tight curly hair, a small mouth and large build. To Sidney, she seemed to be a person who, deliberately or otherwise, looked much older than her age. Perhaps it was merely the absence of make-up or the tweed skirt and granny slippers, but she struck him as a woman who had bypassed the frivolity of youth and was headed full steam to middle age.

'There's not many, to be fair,' Sidney replied to her comment.

'And Eve has employed you to find her sister?'

'That's correct.'

Eleanor gazed out of her window. Beyond the fields, there was a partial view of the sea. Quite pleasant, Sidney thought.

'And you have no idea where Fiona might have gone?' he asked again. He'd first posed the question when Eleanor had opened her front door to him.

'None at all, I'm afraid. Have you asked around the close?'

'Yes, but nobody seems to know. Someone did mention an issue over money?'

'Oh, I'm sure they did,' said Eleanor with the merest hint of a smile. 'Such a vulgar subject, though, don't you think, Mr Valentine?'

'They say it makes the world go round.'

'Mm. But it's not what we're taught at Sunday school.'

Eleanor maintained her gaze out to sea. Sidney's eyes swept around the sitting room. Everything seemed to have its place. All prim and proper. A folded newspaper sat in a rack beneath a polished coffee table. The fire was neatly set with sticks and coal. A pendulum clock on the chimney breast ticked, a model sailing ship in a bottle sat on the mantelpiece, and a budgie chirruped in its cage in the corner. There wasn't a book out of place on the shelves.

'And what do you do, Eleanor?' he asked, realising he was going to learn nothing more about why Fiona had taken her leave of Finn Close.

'I teach history in the high school at Coleraine, Mr Valentine. Hardly as exciting as being a private eye but not without some charm. It is rewarding to play a part in the education of young people.'

'Absolutely. It's certainly a wonderful vocation.'

'Have you always been a detective?'

'No. I began with the navy, moved into security, then insurance investigations before the detective work. But, Eleanor, I've already taken up too much of your time. If there's nothing more you can add about Fiona, I won't keep you any longer.'

Sidney stood up to leave, but Eleanor stayed put.

'You know, Mr Valentine, there are people around here who could help with your inquiry. They probably know where Fiona has gone and certainly know the reason why she has fled.'

'Fled? Is that what it is? Has Fiona left in fear of something?'

'I can't say for sure.'

'How well did you know her?'

'We weren't close friends, merely neighbours. I think that is all we are to each other in Finn Close. Not friends but good neighbours. I like to think that we look out for each other.'

'Did you know Fiona's work colleague, Teddy?'

'She mentioned him from time to time. Besides, Teddy is quite well known in the area. Why do you ask?'

'My daughter and I found him murdered in his home a few hours ago.'

Eleanor gasped, a hand going to her mouth. 'But that's awful! You don't believe that Fiona has something to do with it?'

Chapter 9

Pints of Guinness were set before father and daughter in the saloon bar of the Armada Hotel, busy and noisy with weekenders. There was not a free seat to be had, and several parties had gathered around the bar. If pressed, neither Sidney nor Ursula could have explained why they were remaining in the area. Stumbling on the scene of a murder had complicated what may at first have seemed a straightforward endeavour – finding Eve's sister Fiona. But Sidney and Ursula couldn't help thinking that the two issues were connected.

'Yer woman Eve must be pretty desperate to find her sister if she was prepared to pay so much cash up front,' said Ursula.

Sidney supped his pint then looked pensive as he set his glass back on the table.

'You'd think in this day and age, they would have at least communicated by text,' he said. 'But didn't you say that somebody in Finn Close claimed they were in it together?'

'Yes, whatever *it* is,' said Ursula. 'Do you not think there's something odd about that street?'

'Seems just like any other. Takes all sorts, I suppose.'

'But didn't that woman you spoke to suggest that there were people in the close who know exactly what's been going on with Fiona?'

'She did, aye.'

Sidney's laid-back approach to their investigations was a frequent irritation to Ursula. It didn't have to be a missing person or a murder. He displayed the same horizontal attitude when chasing benefit fraudsters or even counting potholes on a busy road. She sat forward, her elbows on the table, hoping to shake some urgency into her father.

'Well, don't you think we should be finding out who knows what in that street? We can't just go home tomorrow and tell Eve that she was right, her sister has scarpered. We have to find out why. And now there's a dead pirate to be thinking about too!'

Sidney nodded his agreement and took another sip of beer. Ursula, bemused, waited for his words of wisdom. Nothing came.

'Well? What do we do next?' she said, exasperated.

'You can lower your voice for a start. There's already too many people that know why we're here. This is a tight community; word gets around. The murder is a hot topic. I heard the receptionist talking about it on the phone.'

'What do we do next?' she repeated, exaggerating her whisper.

'Until someone in Finn Close is prepared to tell us the reason why Fiona has taken off, we concentrate on Teddy the pirate.'

'That won't be easy,' said Ursula. 'DI Kelso warned us to stay out of it.'

'We'll just have to work under her radar.'

Chapter 10

A brave wind, more than capable of blowing a body from a clifftop, whipped along the coast. The sky was clear, the sun shining, but in this part of the world, it didn't mean anything. An hour from now, the rain could be driving into your face as you marvelled at the curious arrangement of rocks and stones by the Atlantic shore. The Giant's Causeway, the coastline and surrounding cliffs, were under the care of the National Trust. There was a visitor centre and car park for those intending to walk the cliff and coastal footpaths around the peculiar rock formation. In addition to tourist services provided by the National Trust, there were several private enterprises advertising guided tours of the north Antrim coastline.

Sidney had learned from Eve that Fiona worked for one of these companies, and Cissy had told Ursula that Teddy was her colleague. The specific operation, however, proved trickier to pin down. It was a matter of choosing from North Antrim Tours, North Antrim Excursions, Causeway Explorers, Giant's Causeway Walking Tours, Causeway Adventures, Giants, Myths and Legends Tours,

Game of Thrones Guided Tours and finally, Causeway History Tours. Some of these companies had a physical presence close to the car park, while several merely had an advertising board plonked at the roadside showing a website name and a phone number, or, in a few instances, a QR code for making bookings. It was still early morning but, on a Sunday, particularly in reasonably fine weather, there was a steady flow of vehicles into the car park.

Using her mobile, Ursula began checking out the remote operations, while Sidney enquired of the personnel present at the others. It didn't take long to strike gold. Sidney called out to his daughter and surprised by his success, she joined him by a small wooden hut, with a sign on the door displaying the name 'Causeway History Tours'. A slightly built young man in his early twenties with black hair and swarthy face stood next to Sidney holding a bunch of leaflets in his hand.

'This is Gary,' said Sidney. 'Fiona's colleague. Apparently, Teddy was the owner of the business.'

'Hiya,' Ursula chirped.

'Hello,' Gary replied. He looked rather pleadingly at Sidney.

'I didn't know what to do,' he said. 'I heard about Teddy last night. Opening up this morning seemed like the right thing to be doing.'

'Is there anyone else to take charge?' Sidney asked. 'A partner of Teddy's or a family member?'

The young man shook his head.

'Not that I know of. Teddy wasn't married. He never mentioned having any close family. He just ran this business to pass the time. It doesn't make much money. Barely enough to pay Fiona and me.'

'What was Teddy like; was he good to work for?' Sidney asked.

'Great. Everybody liked Teddy. He was a cheerful, friendly guy, and nobody knew more about the Causeway than him.'

'Did he have many friends?' Ursula asked.

'Loads of mates, although I don't know of anyone really close.'

'How about Fiona?' Ursula suggested.

She and Sidney detected a slight hesitation in Gary.

'How did she fit into the operation?' Sidney prompted.

'Oh, right. Fiona was the same as me. She mainly took bookings and handed out leaflets. During busy times, Teddy got her to take some of the tours, and me sometimes, but usually he did them. He was the expert. Fiona only had a passing knowledge that she'd picked up from Teddy, and I know a bit from growing up around here.'

'Were the two of them close?' Ursula asked.

'Friends, I suppose, but not that close. Not like together or anything. Not a couple. At least, I don't think so. I think they got on all right. They argued a bit.'

'What about?' Sidney jumped in.

Again, Gary's hesitation was obvious. It gave rise to a slight stutter.

'D-don't t-think it was anything serious. N-not really. F-Fiona stood up for herself, that's all.'

'But what did they argue about, Gary? Was it about money?' Sidney asked as Ursula tugged his sleeve.

'Trouble coming,' she mumbled.

Sidney turned to see DI Kelso getting out of a police car. She didn't look happy, but then again, the sour expression and clenched lips might well have been her default. It was soon clear that she wasn't about to go through the niceties of a morning's greeting.

'I thought I told you two to sling your hook,' she said.

'Good morning, Detective Inspector Kelso,' said Sidney. 'Nice to see you again, too. And working hard on the weekend, I see.'

The detective's face seemed to stiffen at Sidney's embellished charm. Her companion, a young detective constable, Ursula presumed, cast a beady eye on her as if it

33

were a technique newly learned from his superior. But he was another guy whose gaze found its way to her chest despite its concealment beneath a hoodie.

'Listen, Mr Valentine,' said Kelso. 'I don't want you anywhere near my investigation, is that clear?'

'Perfectly,' Sidney replied with a grin. 'And I'm glad to see you're taking the right approach in coming to Teddy's workplace.'

Kelso stood with hands on hips, looking thoroughly irritated by Sidney. Ursula imagined it wouldn't take much for the cop to arrest them.

'We're just organising a wee tour of the Causeway, isn't that right, Gary?' Ursula said.

Kelso looked from one person to another. It seemed to be a matter of how much leeway to give before losing the rag.

'Right,' she snapped. 'Off you go on your tour. And when you've finished, set your satnav for Belfast and go home. Understand? Detective Constable Brown will stay here to see you off.'

'Ach, sure, there's no need for that. Constable Brown will be frozen stiff out here in the cold,' said Ursula, winking at the officer.

The detective in a dark suit, shirt and tie couldn't help smiling his appreciation of Ursula's apparent concern for his well-being.

'Off you go on your tour,' Kelso repeated.

'Right, let's go, Gary,' said Sidney.

The young guide quickly locked up his hut and strolled off with father and daughter. Kelso and Brown watched them go.

'See you later, Browny love!' Ursula called with a big smile.

Kelso winced while Brown tried to look serious.

'I think that young detective is taken with you,' said Sidney.

'Na, Daddy. Just with my boobs.'

Gary flushed at her remark, but Ursula was undeterred.

'Come on, Gary,' she said, taking his arm. 'Tell us everything about the Giant's Causeway.'

When Sidney glanced behind, as they strolled towards the coastal path, Kelso was still looking on. How long, he thought, before she realises that they have just stolen the one person she had come to interview?

Chapter 11

Gary walked them downhill on a path that skirted around the cliffs at Portnaboe. Several eiders bobbed on the sheltered water of the bay and the piped call of oystercatchers scavenging on the shore competed with the squawking gulls overhead. Passing below the smooth boulders known as the Onion Skin Rocks, they rounded a bend at Windy Gap where they got their first sight of the Causeway. The young lad seemed knowledgeable of the geology of the landscape, reeling off the statistics of the age and magnitude of the famous rock formations.

'Just less than sixty million years ago,' he explained, 'this area was awash with molten lava that cooled and cracked in a zigzag fashion, eventually forming a honeycomb of columns. The result was an array of regular-shaped rocks. If the cooling had occurred in a uniform manner, then all the columns would have had six sides, but some have only four or five, while some have seven, eight or even nine sides. It is estimated that there are around forty thousand columns in this area.' Gary paused as he usually did, just to let the information sink in.

Ursula and Sidney nodded their appreciation, both recalling memories of school field trips to the north Antrim coast. For father and daughter, thirty years apart, it had comprised a study of the many geographical features of the coastline, the raised beaches, cliff stacks, coastal erosion and the famous basalt pillars forming a causeway that stepped into the sea. The legend, of course, was that feuding giants had constructed a highway stretching all the way from Scotland under the sea to Ireland.

They learned that Gary was a lapsed student of archaeology with a particular interest in the ruined castles of the region – Dunseverick, Kinbane and Dunluce. Ursula was keen, however, to hear more about the legend of the giant Finn McCool.

'Is it true that McCool, when he was fighting with the other giant bloke, had a bet on who could claim Ireland first?'

Gary strode on, listening politely to Ursula's recounting of folklore but saying nothing.

'Then McCool cut off his own hand and threw it so he was first to land in Ireland. And that's how we get the red hand of Ulster?'

Gary said nothing. Ursula wanted her answer.

'Well, is that true?'

'Na,' Gary said light-heartedly. 'That story is actually about O'Neill, not McCool, and it was a boat race, but it's only a legend.'

'What about the one where Finn tears a sod from the earth and hurls it at the Scottish giant, but it lands in the sea and becomes the Isle of Man? And the hole left behind became Lough Neagh?'

Gary smiled.

'You're right about there being stories of giants but none of them are true,' he said. 'Many of the names of rock formations around here, like the Giant's Boot, Giant's Coffin and Giant's Cannons, were invented by tour guides back in Victorian times to keep the legend going. Teddy didn't like talking about all that stuff. The Americans lap it up, but he preferred to stick to historical facts. Apart from the geology of the Causeway, he liked to talk about the local castles and the *Girona*.'

'The *Girona*? What's that?' Ursula asked, now standing on the Causeway close to a point where it dipped beneath the waves.

It was a place where you could feel the almighty power of the sea, on a day such as this where a huge swell threatened to swallow all before it. You felt almost that the land was moving too in perfect synchrony with the waves, and you had the inclination to sway in time with it. And yet this strange pavement, formed purely by nature without human hand, had withstood this power for millions of years.

Sidney had heard of the *Girona*. He remembered the name from his school field trip nearly fifty years ago.

'Wasn't that a ship from the Spanish Armada?' he asked.

'It was indeed,' Gary replied, probably relieved to be off the subject of feuding giants. 'She was a galleass ship, which means she was powered by sail and oars.'

Quite enthusiastically, Gary resumed his pointing out of the major features in the vicinity of the Causeway. He then proceeded towards the Organ, an array of basalt pillars within the cliffs and resembling the pipes of a cathedral organ, before taking the Shepherd's Path that led to the top of the cliffs. They strolled eastwards, the cliff edge to their left and heathland to their right.

'Out there,' Gary said, gazing seawards and pointing to a headland below on his right, 'that's Lacada Point and just beyond it is Port na Spaniagh – the spot where the *Girona* went down.'

'Wasn't there supposed to be treasure on board when she sank?' Sidney asked.

'Right again,' Gary replied. 'The ship was overloaded with passengers. Most of them drowned. There were quite a few Spanish noblemen among the officers on board, and the ship carried a lot of their valuables such as gold coins, jewels and religious artefacts. Local people down the years knew of a sunken ship out there, but the wreck wasn't located until the 1960s. Divers recovered a lot of stuff, mostly from the seabed. It's on display at the Ulster Museum in Belfast. Teddy was very interested in the *Girona*.'

'A clever chap then?' Ursula said.

'I suppose he was,' said Gary. 'Although the *Girona* was a bit of an obsession with him. He studied everything about it. The Spanish Armada, Francis Drake, the Tudors, Elizabeth I, Philip II of Spain. He could have written a book on it. To be honest, he tended to bore some of the tourists going on about it. Although plenty of them were really interested in the idea of there being treasure.'

'But it was recovered,' said Ursula. 'You said it's in the museum.'

'Well,' Gary said, drawing out the word, 'Teddy believed there were more valuables to be had.'

'You mean there's still treasure around the wreck?' Sidney asked.

'Possibly. But Teddy had a theory that when the few survivors came ashore, they would have brought some of their most valuable belongings with them. The ship was dashed upon the rocks; so, there would have been debris washed up on the shore too. There may have been valuable items amongst it. Apparently, the survivors had to pay the locals for helping them to make it home to Spain.'

'But surely any gold or jewels would have been used at the time and eventually dispersed. It was over four hundred years ago,' said Sidney.

'I agree. But Teddy was convinced that some of it was kept together. He believed it was paid to a local boy, a chieftain named Sorley Boy MacDonnell from Dunluce Castle, to secure safe passage for the few survivors of the wreck.'

'How much are we talking about?' Ursula asked. They'd stopped on the cliff path directly above Lacada Point gazing over the bay towards Port na Spaniagh.

'No idea, but Teddy reckoned it was substantial. He was convinced that it's still around here somewhere, and he was determined to find it. Never stopped talking about it. Sometimes you could get tired listening to him.'

'Maybe he did find it,' said Sidney.

Chapter 12

Ursula was merrily eating her way through a traditional Sunday lunch of roast beef, potatoes and Yorkshire pudding. Sidney, too, was enjoying the fayre served at the Armada Hotel.

'So, do you think that Teddy had found this treasure from the *Girona*, and somebody murdered him to get hold of it?' she asked her father.

He set down his knife and fork and took a sip of his fruity red wine.

'That history teacher, Eleanor Martinez, suggested that others in Finn Close know what's been going on with Fiona. And you told me that the old couple mentioned money.'

'You think they really meant treasure?'

'Possibly.'

'So that would mean Fiona killed Teddy to get her hands on the loot and took off without telling her sister.'

'Possibly.'

'Fiona would have known about the treasure too because, according to Gary, Teddy was never done talking about it.'

'Possibly.'

'Don't feel that you have to commit to a definitive answer,' said Ursula.

She paused for a moment and put down her knife and fork.

'There's just one teeny tiny wee small detail that's bugging me,' she said.

'And what's that?'

'Why was Teddy dressed as a pirate?'

'Shut up and eat your dinner,' said Sidney.

* * *

Sidney was sitting by a roaring fire, feet outstretched, eyes closed, but not asleep, and nursing a glass of Black Bush in his hand. He'd insisted upon a walk to the distillery after lunch. Established in 1608, the world's oldest licensed whiskey distillery was only a quarter of a mile up the road from the hotel. The whiskey tour had put him in the mood for a tipple when he got back. This was, of course, in addition to what he'd sampled on the tour. It was the second Baileys of the evening for Ursula as she browsed her phone, texting her girlfriends, reading various news apps and looking up information on the sinking of the *Girona*.

A party of four guests, two middle-aged couples, sat at a nearby table discussing the events surrounding the murder of the Causeway tour guide. Ursula knew her father was earwigging the conversation. She too had learned that the group were not locals but weekend guests from Belfast. What useful information Sidney would get out of their musings was debatable, but Ursula thought it best not to disturb him.

'Somebody from round here has done it,' said one of the women with permed hair and a pink cardigan. 'It's nearly always somebody local.'

'Or someone within the family,' said the second woman in a gruff city tone. 'A *domestic*, they call it.'

'It's awful bad when you can't come away for a quiet weekend without some poor soul getting topped,' the first continued.

One of the gents laughed. 'Now, how has it spoiled your weekend? Sure, it wasn't any of us who got murdered.'

'A pity it wasn't you, Sammy,' the woman hit back. 'Give my head some peace.'

The second male joined in.

'Calm down, Molly,' he said, 'or there will be a flaming domestic.'

Sidney opened his eyes, a smile spreading over his face. He looked at Ursula.

'That's something we haven't considered,' he whispered. 'That Teddy's murder was simply a domestic.'

'Doesn't explain the missing Fiona,' Ursula replied. 'Unless they were romantically involved, although Eve told us that Fiona didn't have a boyfriend.'

'You're always putting obstacles in the way, daughter.'

'So, what do we do tomorrow? We can't just head home, not after there's been a murder and us thinking it has something to do with our case.'

'I was dreading you saying that.' Sidney sat upright and polished off the remainder of his whiskey. 'I reckon we have a lot more questions to ask in that cul-de-sac. Don't forget, it's technically this Fiona woman we're here to find. Solving a murder is a job for the police.'

'You've changed your tune. So, we're not going to think about poor Teddy?'

'Since we reckon the two are linked, we do both. If the cops have finished at that wee cottage, I wouldn't mind another look around Teddy's place.'

Chapter 13

'DI Kelso will blow a gasket if she catches us out here,' said Ursula.

Her concerns prompted Sidney to suggest that they leave their van at the Causeway car park, walk back along the road then turn right into the lane leading to Teddy's cottage.

The morning was overcast although it felt warmer than the previous day. Sidney moved slowly, well fuelled with an Ulster fry for breakfast. Ursula, after two days in a hotel, was nearing the point where she couldn't manage another bite. She was still full after her Sunday lunch, and this morning had struggled with just cornflakes and coffee at breakfast. She marched ahead of her father and was first to spot the police incident tape stretched across the gateway to Teddy's property. Thankfully, there were no police vehicles around or any indication that the cottage was being guarded. It was, however, designated as a crime scene, and they would be breaking the law if they strayed beyond the cordon.

'What do you think, Daddy?' she said, as they paused at the tape.

'Hopefully, we'll find that the peelers haven't bothered to lock all the doors. They probably believe that a strip of police tape casts an invisible force field around the house.'

The pair ducked beneath the blue-and-white tape and proceeded to the front door of the cottage.

'Wrong!' chirped Ursula, trying the door handle. 'It's locked.'

Sidney was already stepping around to the back. When Ursula reached him, he was shaking the handle of the back door as if it were his divine right that it should be unlocked.

Ursula laughed. 'What now, old man?'

She'd scarcely uttered her jibe before Sidney had lifted a broom that was leaning against the wall and rammed the handle at one of the quarter panes of the kitchen window. Glass tinkled. Sidney reached his hand inside the hole and released the catch.

'All yours,' he said, intimating that Ursula should climb inside and open the back door.

'Breaking and entering in addition to crossing a police cordon,' she said.

'The peelers will think it happened during their investigation,' Sidney said.

'You have a very low opinion of local law enforcement.'

Ursula clambered onto the sill then manoeuvred her body through the open window. Seconds later, she'd dropped to the kitchen floor and opened the door for Sidney.

'We need to be quick,' he said. 'And keep an eye out for the charming DI Kelso. I'd prefer another night in the Armada Hotel rather than Coleraine police station.'

Ursula took the upstairs, while Sidney began in the kitchen.

He opened cupboards to find only crockery, a sandwich maker and some items of food: tea, coffee, cereal, cans of beans and soups. The drawers next to the white sink held cutlery, several batteries and a torch. Looking around, Sidney could see few places where anything of interest might be lurking and, if asked, he would have difficulty explaining exactly what he was looking for. He came to the lounge, the door wide open, and stepped inside. His attention was drawn immediately to the picture on the wall above the fireplace. Now, following the conversation with tour guide Gary, he assumed that he was staring at a picture of the galleass

Girona in full sail, riding a stormy ocean. Things hadn't ended well for the ship.

Sidney turned next to the bookcase and again his interest was piqued by many of the books relating to historic ships, shipwrecks and histories of the Spanish Armada and other naval battles. One book had the same image of a sailing ship on the dustcover as the picture on the lounge wall. He leafed through the hardback book noticing the many comments scribbled in the margins. There were dates, notes and cross-references to other pages. Sidney couldn't begin to understand it all, but it occurred to him that the police who'd presumably searched the cottage had no clue either.

At the foot of the bookcase, he pulled open a large drawer.

'Bingo!' he mumbled to himself, looking down upon a collection of maps and sea charts. 'X marks the spot, perhaps.'

No such luck. Again, Sidney had no firm idea what he was looking at. Some of the maps were pristine and uncreased by folds. On others, lines had been drawn in pencil or ink. Some of it resembled attempts at triangulation, and amongst it, he recognised the outline of the north Antrim coast. He closed the drawer, but as he did so, he noticed a couple of books about metal detection and the search for Roman and Anglo-Saxon treasure in East Anglia. There was a built-in cupboard to the right of the chimney breast, the doors held closed with a hook and eye fastening. Inside, he found an upright Hoover and next to it, a metal detector – further confirmation that Teddy had been engaged in a treasure hunt. Sidney knew little about such devices, but it looked quite an expensive model. It seemed that young Gary hadn't been wrong regarding his boss. Teddy had been engrossed in serious research. Whether he had been successful, Sidney couldn't yet say, but the finding of treasure had always been a strong motive for murder.

He heard a clatter of feet on the staircase and stepped from the lounge back into the kitchen.

Ursula tumbled right into him. 'Peelers! Time we weren't here.'

She grabbed her father by the arm and ushered him towards the back door. Once outside, Sidney peered around the corner of the cottage. A marked police car had stopped at its own cordon.

'This way,' Ursula whispered.

There was a narrow gap between gorse bushes that bordered a field. It was the only way to avoid being seen by the police. Ursula tugged Sidney across the garden, through the gap and into the field. They waited behind the cover of the bushes, Ursula stealing a glimpse of the activity at the cottage.

'Find anything?' she whispered to Sidney.

'Not much. Confirmation, I suppose, that Teddy had an interest in local history and the story of the *Girona*. How about you?'

'Depends.'

'What do you mean, it depends?'

She had another glance towards the cottage. A second police car had arrived, and Ursula spotted the now familiar figure of DI Kelso climbing out.

'They could be here for a while,' she whispered. 'Time to go. We can skirt around the edge of this field. I don't think anyone will see us.'

'Lead on,' said Sidney not relishing a hike through the countryside. 'Tell me what you found.'

They trampled through damp grass, staying close to the bramble and gorse at the edge. Sidney grimaced. Their route was taking them towards the sea and the cliffs and further from their van. Ursula detected her father's irritation.

'Don't worry, we can double back once we're out of sight of the cops.'

'Just slow down a bit. We're not on a flaming route march. And will you please tell me what you found in the cottage?'

She stopped and pulled a slip of paper from her pocket.

'I found this in a bedside drawer. It's a list of numbers. Could mean something, map coordinates maybe, if he was searching for treasure, or perhaps bank account numbers?'

Sidney examined the twenty or so numbers that looked as though they'd been scribbled down in haste. Some digits appeared bunched, perhaps to denote a single number, while others were in isolation. He struggled to make sense of them. He thought of the charts he'd found in the drawer of the bookcase. Common sense suddenly took hold. He winced and handed the note back to Ursula.

'Might just be a list of his lottery numbers,' he said with a titter and marched on.

Ursula looked at the paper, tut-tutted then stuffed it into her pocket and followed Sidney.

'There was also an interesting collection of clothing in his wardrobe,' she said. 'It seems that Teddy liked dressing up, and not just as a pirate. There was a clown outfit and a lot of leather gear.'

Chapter 14

Exhausted from his physical activity of the morning – having to flee Teddy's cottage, escape across a field, skirt the clifftops and double back to where they'd left the van – Sidney insisted on a return to the hotel for a coffee and a sit-down. Ursula didn't argue. She knew it was pointless. A coffee-infused father was always preferable to a ratty, caffeine-deficient one. Over the refreshments, Sidney remained quiet. Ursula knew he was thinking. At times, it was merely him daydreaming, but she reckoned they had gathered sufficient information to induce some serious thought. Ursula had a go too but quickly resorted to browsing her phone. She tried to learn more about the four-hundred-year-old story of the wreck of the *Girona*.

'What do you think about Teddy the pirate then?' she asked, aware she was disturbing Sidney's ponderings.

'I don't think getting an answer to that will help us find Fiona.'

'Do you reckon she's still alive? Whoever killed Teddy may have also killed Fiona. That's if she's not the perpetrator.'

'Why? That is the question,' said Sidney.

'Who are you, Shakespeare's wee brother?'

'What I mean is that if we can find out why Fiona has disappeared, we'll probably find out where she's gone and why Teddy was murdered. The two things must be connected.'

Ursula didn't dispute her father's logic.

'Then we need to get back to Finn Close and get one of its residents to spill the beans,' she said. 'According to you, Eleanor Martinez was adamant that her neighbours know exactly what's been going on.'

'Yes, and I wonder if they might be more forthcoming now that news of a murder is all over the place. Or possibly less so if one of them is the killer.'

'Cissy and Bertie are a good place to start,' said Ursula. 'They were first to mention the issue of money.'

* * *

They didn't get as far as Finn Close, however, before encountering one of its residents. When they stepped from the hotel into Main Street in Bushmills, Ursula spotted a man she had been eager to speak to again. Sidney had no clue what was happening when she darted across the road. A postman was plodding along, delivering mail to several shops and pushing envelopes through the letter boxes of private houses. A post office van was parked fifty yards away. Ursula wanted to nab him before the guy had the chance to climb in and drive off.

'Excuse me!' she called, running to catch up.

The postman turned around. He had a puzzled look on an otherwise downbeat face.

Ursula reached him and smiled. 'You live at Finn Close, number three, next door to Fiona, don't you?'

The man showed no signs of recognising or remembering her. He stared but didn't speak. He was the guy that Ursula had disturbed from his sleep.

'Sorry to have bothered you the other day. But I'm still looking for Fiona. Just wondering if you had seen or heard from her?'

'No. Why should I?' He made to walk on, but Ursula stepped into his path. 'Do you mind? I've work to do,' he said.

She could tell he didn't like her; maybe her breasts – the spot where his gaze now rested – but not her as a person, a woman trying to be friendly.

'So have I, sunshine,' she said. 'A man has been murdered. Teddy McNaughten. He worked with Fiona, and I reckon somebody who lives in Finn Close knows exactly why she has disappeared.'

'Who are you, the police?'

'I'm a friend of Fiona's sister.'

'In that case, I don't have to tell you anything.'

'So, you do know something about Fiona?'

The man flinched. Suddenly, he looked in a quandary or at least resigned to having to answer the woman who was blocking his way.

'I'm sure Fiona is fine,' he said. 'We're dealing with it.' He knocked into Ursula's shoulder as he marched off.

'What do you mean?' she called after him. 'Who's dealing with it?'

The man didn't look back, and a few yards further on, he ducked into a butcher's shop.

Sidney had witnessed the exchange between Ursula and the postman. He was standing by their van when Ursula re-crossed the street.

'That didn't seem like a friendly meeting,' he said.

'Never mind him. We need to get to Finn Close. Postman Pat more or less admitted that something *is* going on and it involves Fiona.'

Chapter 15

There appeared to be little activity about the cul-de-sac when they arrived. Remaining in the van, avoiding a biting wind sweeping off the Atlantic, Sidney rested his eyes while Ursula kept watch. They had yet to meet Natalie who lived at number four. There was no reply when Ursula had called again, although the green Mini still sat in the driveway. She considered trying Curtis and Julie at number one again to see if they would be more helpful. Maybe they'd hidden behind their apparent domestic row to avoid telling her anything before. Their car wasn't in their driveway, however, so that left the people who had at least welcomed them into their homes, Eleanor the history teacher, and Cissy and Bertie. Friendly yes, but had they really provided anything useful to help track down Fiona?

Ursula nudged her father. 'Wake up, Daddy. Cissy and Bertie have just arrived home.'

They watched as Cissy got out of her car and waddled up the sloping drive to her front door. Bertie was left to retrieve shopping from the boot and to ferry several bags up to the house. Sidney and Ursula waited another ten minutes before calling on the couple.

'Come on in,' Cissy beamed. 'You're just in time for afternoon tea.'

'Ach thanks, Cissy,' Ursula said. 'Sorry for disturbing you again but we have a few more questions to ask, if you don't mind.'

Sidney grinned at Ursula as they stepped inside. The prospect of a cuppa always had Sidney on the up. Ursula introduced her father to Cissy and Bertie, and all four of them were soon seated around the kitchen table, piping hot tea, a plate of ham sandwiches and an enticing Victoria sponge set before them.

Not wishing to overwhelm the couple with probing questions from the outset, Ursula began with small talk. It might still be helpful, she hoped, and would seem less intrusive.

'So, what did you work at before you retired, Bertie?' she asked.

'Farming, love. All my life. My father and grandfather before me,' Bertie replied rather proudly.

'Hard work,' Sidney commented.

'Aye, it was that. But sure, you couldn't beat the outdoor life.'

'Our son, Walter, runs the farm now,' Cissy added. 'Bertie still pops over to lend a hand. We moved here to give Walter and his wee family a bit of space. We let them have the big house. We were going to build something for ourselves on the land, but somehow Bertie never got around to it.' Cissy rolled her eyes at her husband.

'All in good time, Cissy,' said Bertie with a chuckle.

The wife rolled her eyes again.

Sidney had noticed the model of a sailing ship standing on the pine dresser.

'I see you have a model of the *Girona*,' he said to Bertie.

'I do indeed,' Bertie replied. 'But that's not her. That's the *Trinidad Valencera*. She was another casualty from the Armada, wrecked off the coast. Come and see.'

Bertie led Sidney firstly to view the eighteen-inch-high model on the dresser, then padded from the kitchen to the lounge. Set upon a large occasional table in one corner was an intricate wooden model of the *Girona* with full rigging and oars extended.

'There she is,' said Bertie, beaming. 'Made her myself when I was a lad.'

'She's wonderful,' said Sidney, gazing over the ship. 'Very detailed. Takes a lot of skill and patience to make something as good as that.'

'Does indeed,' said Bertie. 'Had some help from my father, of course. He was the expert in wood carving and the man with all the skill.'

'Did he have an interest in the *Girona*?'

'Oh boys, aye. I was raised with all the stories of the Causeway. You see, the family farm is close to the water where the wreck was discovered in the sixties. We witnessed all the commotion when those diver boys brought the treasure ashore.'

'I take it you knew Teddy McNaughten?'

'Did indeed. Bit of a fanatic about the *Girona* was Teddy.'

'Do you know of any reason why someone would want to kill him?'

A grave expression appeared on the old man's face.

'Boyso, that's a bad business altogether. Can't think why anyone would wish to hurt poor Teddy.'

* * *

Left in the kitchen with Cissy, Ursula attempted to get some answers to the mystery enveloping this small part of the world.

'What's with the woman at number four? I haven't got any answer, but there's a car parked in the drive.'

'Natalie? Oh, she comes and goes, that one.'

'Does she usually leave her car at home?' Ursula asked.

'I don't keep tabs on the woman. Not my kind of person, if you know what I mean, Ursula.'

'I'm sorry, but I don't.'

'Well, she's divorced, isn't she. I mean, women like that.'

Ursula grinned her understanding but thought it best not to comment. Cissy's attitude was that of an old-fashioned puritanical breed. The idea of divorce would be abhorrent to a woman like her. They were most likely views instilled from an early age and born of a strict religious upbringing. Ursula decided to steer the subject away from women of dubious morals.

'Last time I was here, you mentioned something about money going missing.'

'Did I, love? I don't remember.'

'You said that Fiona had gone and taken the money with her. Whose money were you talking about?'

'Oh, take no heed of what I say, love.'

'But?'

Sidney reappeared with Bertie, and it seemed Cissy was off the hook as far as answering Ursula's question was concerned. Ursula detected the relief sweeping over the woman's face.

'Did you see Bertie's ship, Mr Valentine?' Cissy asked brightly.

'Very impressive,' Sidney replied, looking at Ursula.

She frowned to indicate she'd got nothing from Cissy. Sidney gave a barely perceptible shrug to suggest he'd had little success also. But Ursula wasn't finished with the old woman.

'Cissy,' she said, 'have you any idea why Teddy would have been dressed as a pirate when he was killed?'

It seemed she'd just sent the woman's limited imagination into meltdown. If she hadn't already offended her sensitivities in discussing Natalie, she had now. Cissy glanced at her husband then stared rather disgustedly at Ursula.

'Sounds very strange, love, but I would have no idea why he would be dressed in such a fashion.'

'A fancy-dress party nearby, maybe?' Ursula was playing now, and Cissy's hospitality was beginning to wear thin. It was doubtful that Ursula would ever be invited back for more home-baked scones or Victoria sponge.

'Not that I heard of,' Cissy replied, minus her smile.

They soon took their leave of the couple and, finding no one else at home in the close, they decided to head back to the hotel. As they drove away, Sidney and Ursula agreed that since they had gained little from their latest visit to Finn Close, they should perhaps admit defeat and return home the following day.

When Ursula reached the junction of the lane with Causeway Road, several police vehicles, their lights flashing and sirens blaring, raced by. They watched as the convoy left the main road and headed towards the Causeway visitor centre.

Chapter 16

Sidney and Ursula realised that if DI Kelso was among the gathering of police officers in the car park at the Causeway visitor centre, she would not be pleased to see them driving in. But once their curiosity was aroused, father and daughter were never inclined to worry about incurring police displeasure.

Before the police had time to establish an exclusion zone, Ursula pulled into the car park of the Causeway Hotel, a splendid whitewashed building that dominated the headland. They stopped a few yards from three police cars and a forensics van. There were plenty of onlookers gathered outside the visitor centre which was only a few yards from the hotel, so Sidney and Ursula hoped they wouldn't be noticed if they were to mingle. People were chatting amongst themselves, and several pointed towards the path that led down below the cliffs to the Causeway.

Ursula spotted DI Kelso getting out of a car. She didn't look happy, but Ursula didn't read much into it. The detective could be dealing with a robbery, an assault, a dead body or a child who'd had their ice cream stolen; Kelso would have the same expression. Then, to Ursula's shock and surprise, Sidney sidled right up to the detective and started a conversation. When Kelso's hands went to her hips, Ursula reckoned her father was only seconds from being arrested. But suddenly Kelso turned away and marched off. Sidney came over to Ursula.

'She wouldn't tell me anything,' he said.

'Some of these people seem to know what's been happening,' Ursula said. 'I'll try to join in.'

She wandered off, meandering through the gathering of people now held at bay by a strip of police incident tape stretching across the path to the Causeway.

'What's going on?' she announced, more than asked, to no one in particular.

A man in his forties, holding the hand of a woman of similar age, turned around. 'There's a body down there,' he said.

'On the Causeway,' said his companion, her free hand tugging nervously at the drawstring of her anorak.

'Male or female?' Ursula asked.

'It's a woman,' said another male voice. 'She was just lying there.'

'Dead?' asked another woman.

The question was followed by a lot of mumbled discussion. Ursula decided that no one really knew much beyond what she'd already heard. Sidney grabbed her arm and led her away from the onlookers and the police who were now clearing a space for the vehicles to drive down the path. There were more people arriving in the car park, having been down at the Causeway when the body was discovered and then moved on by the police.

'We'll go along the clifftop, maybe get a better view,' said Sidney. 'Hopefully, we can get closer to the scene before the cops notice us.'

They hurried along the trail on the cliff edge then started down the steps on the Shepherd's Path. The day was beginning to close in, the thick clouds overhead looking more ominous as the light faded.

Unfortunately, for Sidney and Ursula, an alert constable had already decided the approach to the Causeway via the clifftop was a route that needed to be sealed off. No doubt his quick thinking would earn him a pat on the back from DI Kelso. He greeted them halfway down the steps to the shore.

'This area is closed to the public,' he announced. 'You'll have to return to the car park by the way you came.' He nodded towards the top of the steps.

'What's going on?' Ursula asked, feigning innocence.

'It's a police matter.'

Sidney was straining to see all the way to the Causeway. He watched several officers clambering over the rocks close to the water's edge. Following behind were a couple of others carrying what looked like a white incident tent. He didn't see anything that could be a body, but the police were looking busy, and more were arriving in cars at the turning circle beside the famous rocks.

With nothing to do but retrace their steps, Sidney and Ursula had reached similar conclusions.

'I wonder if they've just found our missing Fiona,' said Sidney.

'Poor Eve. How are we going to break the news?'

Chapter 17

Ursula sprawled on Sidney's bed, while he stood by the window trying to call Eve McCabe. Regardless of the generous retainer she'd paid for their services, the woman was proving every bit as elusive as her missing sister. She hadn't answered any of Sidney's calls or responded to voicemail messages.

'Still no answer,' he said. 'It would be better that Eve heard it from us rather than on the news. We're the people who are supposed to be looking for her sister.'

'What do you think has happened, Daddy?'

'Well, we don't know yet if she's been murdered. It might have been an accident.'

'But considering how that crowd at Finn Close are behaving, there has to be something fishy going on.'

Sidney retrieved another number from his contact list and pressed 'call'.

'Hello,' he said. 'Could I speak to DI Kelso please?'

Ursula sat upright. This was going to be good. Surprisingly, Sidney had some success. Immediately, he switched to speakerphone to let Ursula to hear the conversation.

'Sorry to bother you, Inspector Kelso.'

'Who's this?' she said curtly.

'It's Sidney Valentine.'

There was a pause before she asked her next question. 'Do I know you?'

Sidney explained who he was and before the police detective could object, he stated the reason for calling.

'I just want to know if the body you found at the Causeway this afternoon is Fiona McCabe?'

The cop sounded taken aback that Sidney had had the audacity to call her.

'I thought I told you, Mr Valentine, to keep your nose out of police business.'

'Now where's the harm, DI Kelso? I'm back home just like you told me. I merely wish to inform my client if the body you found is her sister.'

The detective was close to yelling now.

'Mr Valentine, I know exactly where you are. You've been skulking at the Armada Hotel in Bushmills with that irritating daughter of yours and poking your nose into my investigation.'

Sidney looked at Ursula. Her mouth had dropped open at being described as irritating. But Sidney was more surprised that the police had been keeping an eye on them.

'For the last time, Mr Valentine, go home and leave the detective work to the professionals.'

'So, is that a yes to the body being Fiona McCabe?' Sidney tried again.

'Go away, sir.' The call was cut.

'She's not very nice, Daddy, telling us to leave investigating to the professionals.'

'I know, love. And you're not that irritating.'

'Gee, thanks.' She threw herself backwards on the bed. 'So, what now?'

'It's time we paid a visit to the Garden of Eden.'

* * *

Two hours later, Sidney and Ursula were standing on yet another doorstep getting nil response from ringing a doorbell. It was of no real surprise. The bungalow was in darkness and there wasn't a car in the driveway, although they couldn't be sure if Eve owned one. Sidney tried calling the woman on his phone again, but it continued to revert to voicemail.

'I'd love to know what's going on with that woman,' said Ursula. 'She asks us to find her sister then disappears herself and doesn't reply to our calls.'

'If it wasn't for the two and a half grand that she paid us, I would pack this case in. It's getting messier by the minute.'

'We may as well head home. DI Kelso won't be happy if she finds us back in Bushmills. Until we contact Eve and get confirmation that the woman's body found on the Causeway is Fiona, there's little more we can do.'

Sidney agreed, but as Ursula drove them away from Eden, his phone rang. Immediately, he put the caller on speakerphone.

'Mr Valentine, so sorry I missed your calls,' said Eve. She sounded flustered and out of breath but didn't offer an explanation for having ignored them. 'I heard about the woman's body being found at the Giant's Causeway...' Her voice trailed off into sobs.

'We don't yet know if it's your sister,' said Sidney. 'The police haven't released a name.'

'But it must be Fiona,' Eve cried.

'Please try not to think that for now,' said Sidney, trying to sound positive. 'Are you at home now? We've just called at your house, but we can go back again. We really need to update you on what we've found.'

There was silence, and Sidney and Ursula looked at each other.

'No, I'm not at home,' Eve replied, sounding hesitant.

'Where are you? Can you get to our place tomorrow?'

Again, there was silence.

'Eve? Are you there?' said Sidney.

'I'll come to yours,' she replied then cut the call.

'Something's going on with that woman,' said Ursula, 'and I don't think it's just worrying about her sister.'

Chapter 18

Sidney and Ursula were getting ready for bed when the door buzzer sounded. It was approaching midnight, and they had not expected Eve to call that very evening. Having been so elusive, it was odd that she was suddenly keen to meet with the detectives she'd hired. When Ursula opened the door, she was faced with a rather haggard-looking Eve in a crumpled anorak over a faded T-shirt, her eyes red and puffy, her hair in need of brushing.

'I'm sorry it's so late, but you did say it was urgent.'

'Come in,' said Ursula. 'I'll make some tea. You look as though you could do with it.'

Eve followed Ursula into the flat and sat gingerly upon their sofa. Her eyes seemed enormous behind her huge frames, and she gazed apprehensively at Sidney, who appeared to be intent upon an interrogation. He pulled a footstool close to Eve and sat down. Ursula handed her a mug of strong tea.

'For now,' Sidney began in a gentle tone, 'let's continue to believe that Fiona is still alive.'

The woman didn't look as though she believed that but allowed Sidney to proceed.

'What can you tell us about Fiona and Teddy McNaughten?'

'What do you mean?'

'Were they close friends or maybe involved with each other romantically?' Sidney asked.

'I don't think so. That is, I don't really know. Fiona probably wouldn't have told me if she had been.'

'Several of Fiona's neighbours hinted that there was an issue over money and that's the reason Fiona has disappeared. Do you know anything about that?'

Eve sipped her tea. Ursula guessed the woman was stalling and wasn't impressed.

'You hired us to find Fiona,' she chided. 'You paid us a lot of money up front. It's wasted if you can't be honest with us, Eve.'

'I really don't know anything about her neighbours or money,' Eve said. 'Fiona disappeared; that's why I'm paying you to find her. The reasons behind her going don't matter as long as you find her safe and well.'

Sidney winced but changed tack.

'Why have you been so difficult to contact?' he asked. 'Seems to me, Eve, that you are hiding something from us about your motives for finding your sister.'

The woman broke down in tears. Ursula passed her tissues but was unmoved by the display.

Eve sniffed. 'If you don't want to do the job,' she said, 'I'll find someone else, unless my sister is dead.'

Sidney rubbed his face with both hands. It would be so easy to tell the woman they were done.

'We'll continue for now,' he said with a heavy sigh. 'But you must stay in touch with us, Eve. Answer our calls. Don't keep anything from us. If Fiona is alive then we'll find her.'

'Thank you, Mr Valentine. I'm so sorry for any trouble.'

While they drank their tea, Ursula and Sidney tried in vain to extract more information from the woman. Even the smallest detail might prove invaluable. But Eve gave little. She admitted to knowing many of the names of Fiona's neighbours but denied being acquainted with any of them. She confessed to having met Teddy a couple of times but insisted that she knew nothing about him and Fiona being romantically involved, if they were. Finally, Sidney asked a question that had continued to bother him ever since they'd taken the case on.

'Why did you not report that Fiona was missing to the police? You told us that you had.'

Eve dropped her gaze, sipped her tea, removed her glasses and wiped her eyes.

'Is Fiona mixed up in something illegal? Are you frightened of getting her into trouble?'

'I was trying to avoid the publicity. I didn't want the world to know that Fiona has disappeared,' Eve said.

'Why was that? Sidney asked.

'It hardly matters now that a body has been found.'

Chapter 19

Still at home in Holywood, Ursula was preparing breakfast when the local news bulletin came on TV. The headline concerned the discovery of a woman's body at the Giant's Causeway. She called Sidney who was in the bathroom. By the time he'd darted into the kitchen, the item had finished.

'Any name?' he asked, wiping shaving soap from his face with a towel.

'Not yet.'

Sidney slumped into his recliner by the window and stared vacantly over the lough.

'What is going on up there?' he said.

Ursula brought him his tea and a plate with toast.

'One murder, another death possibly connected, and Fiona McCabe is still missing,' Sidney continued.

'Either that makes her a possible victim or the prime suspect,' said Ursula. 'Although, did Eve's attitude not strike you as odd last night? She gave a peculiar answer when we asked her why she hadn't reported Fiona's disappearance to the police.'

'Yes, very strange. You'd have thought that publicity would be just the thing to help find a missing person.'

'Seems like we need a return trip to the north coast,' said Ursula. 'But this time we must find out what the other residents of Finn Close seem reluctant to share with us.'

'Surely now, at least one of the neighbours would be willing to tell us what's been going on.'

* * *

They reached Finn Close by midday. Before leaving home, Ursula had again booked them into the Armada Hotel. They weren't inclined to worry about the police noting their return to Bushmills. Sidney reckoned DI Kelso would be run off her feet having two mysterious deaths to investigate.

The cul-de-sac appeared quiet.

This was a weekday. Those residents like Eleanor and Postman Pat, who had jobs, were presumably at work. Cissy and Bertie didn't seem to be at home. That left Natalie, whom they had yet to meet, and the squabbling couple, Curtis and Julie. They got no reply from Natalie's house, the green Mini still in the drive. Their knock on the blue door of number one was answered, however, and Sidney and Ursula were confronted by a scowling Julie. Her hair wrapped in a towel and moisturising cream on her face, she greeted them with a single word.

'What?'

'Hello, Julie? Isn't that right?' said Ursula with her best-friend smile on show.

'What do you want?' the young woman snapped.

'You might remember us,' Ursula continued. 'We're looking for Fiona McCabe.'

'Can't help you.'

Julie attempted to close her door. It met Sidney's foot.

'Hold on, before you rush off,' he said sternly.

Julie's face may have coloured with anger, but it was impossible to tell beneath her face pack. She glared at Sidney.

'I told you. I don't know anything.'

Ursula produced the bag of white powder that had dropped from Curtis's pocket during her previous visit.

'I was thinking Curtis might have been looking for this.'

Julie's eyes widened, and she reached out her hand to take the bag from Ursula.

'Not so fast,' said Ursula. 'I think perhaps I should hand it in at the police station. Tell them where I found it.'

'No, please, you mustn't,' said Julie in alarm.

'Teddy McNaughten has been murdered, and he was Fiona's boss,' said Sidney. 'I think there is something going on amongst all of you in this close and it's connected with Fiona's disappearance. We're hoping that she hasn't been murdered too. Surely, you don't want to see anyone else get hurt.'

'But it's all her fault,' said Julie, now sounding rather disconsolate.

'Maybe you could explain?' said Sidney.

Julie seemed to consider the suggestion then finally opened her door wide.

'You better come in,' she muttered.

As they stepped into the hallway, Ursula noticed a picture on the wall. Hanging with several framed photos of family or friends, was a small print of an old sailing ship. She could not identify it as the *Girona* but thought it intriguing that another of the homes they'd visited recently had such a picture. Ursula and her father sat together on a low sofa, while Julie remained standing, looking indignant with her arms folded. The friendship reading hadn't risen above frosty, but Sidney and Ursula were well used to uncooperative people. The chances of tea or coffee were even lower than the friendliness rating, but at least they had the woman's attention.

'Maybe you can start by telling us what exactly *is* Fiona's fault?' said Sidney.

'I never did trust her,' Julie replied. 'Too flipping smart, and sly, as it turns out.'

'What did she do?' Ursula asked.

'She's bogged off with all the money!'

'Whose money has she taken?' Sidney asked.

It seemed they were never going to get beyond that basic statement. Sidney and Ursula needed details.

'Everybody's!' Julie continued to bark her answers.

'You're going to have to be more specific, Julie,' said Ursula.

The young woman appeared to be reconsidering allowing strangers asking probing questions into her home.

'Listen, I don't know who or what you are. I'm not telling you anything more until you can prove you're not cops or crooks. How do I know Fiona's sister sent you? The flaming woman could be in on it too.'

Ursula produced a business card from the back pocket of her jeans and gave it to Julie.

'Doesn't prove anything,' Julie said after reading it.

'Then you're going to have to trust us, Julie love,' said Ursula. 'We're trying to find Fiona and since we've started, two people have died. This is now way bigger than whatever reason you might have not to help us.'

Sighing heavily, Julie slumped into an armchair.

'Curtis is going to kill me for telling you this.'

'Please, start at the beginning,' said Sidney. 'Maybe you'll feel better getting it off your chest.'

'Fiona looked after our syndicate.'

Chapter 20

Julie left the room for a few minutes. When she returned, the cream on her face and the towel from her head were gone, revealing damp blonde hair. Sidney and Ursula waited patiently for the woman to continue her story, but it was as though they weren't even in the room as Julie's attention was firmly upon her mobile phone. Before either father or daughter broke the silence, Julie set her phone down on the arm of the chair.

'Right,' she announced, 'Curtis says I can tell you about Fiona as long as you don't tell anyone that it was me. Especially not the cops. And he wants his gear back.' She looked at her visitors, awaiting their agreement.

'OK, we'll try our best to do that,' said Sidney. 'But if this information is linked to the recent deaths, we might have to share it with the police. And we'll hold on to the drugs for now.'

Julie scowled. 'If the cops come to my door, I'll deny everything.'

'You can try,' said Sidney.

'Tell us about this syndicate,' said Ursula, eager to hear the story.

'It's a lottery syndicate,' Julie replied.

'And?'

'We reckon we've won a fortune, but Fiona has taken the money.'

'You're certain that you've won?' Sidney asked.

'Fairly sure, yes. I don't have a note of the numbers because they were different every week and Fiona didn't always share them with us.'

'Then how do you know that you are winners?' asked Ursula.

'Bertie said that he thought we'd won. He told Curtis about meeting Fiona, and she was acting very strange and very nervous. He asked her about that week's lottery draw, joking about becoming a millionaire. She claimed that she hadn't checked the numbers then made some excuse to rush home. The next day, she was gone.'

Ursula glanced at her father. She guessed that he wasn't buying Julie's tale.

'Who else was a member of this syndicate?' he asked.

'Curtis and me, Bertie and Cissy, Natalie at number four, Teddy McNaughten and Fiona. I think maybe Fiona's sister was in it too, but Fiona wasn't always upfront about who was in and who was out.'

'What do you mean?' said Ursula.

'Well, Eugene at number three, for instance.'

Ursula now had a first name for the man she'd labelled Postman Pat.

'One week he was in, the next he was out,' Julie continued. 'Fiona had trouble getting entry money out of him. And she only mentioned her sister once when she asked us if it was OK for her to take part, seeing as she didn't live nearby. Didn't matter to us, I told her, as long as she paid her entry money.'

'So that was everyone in Finn Close, plus Teddy and Fiona's sister who were members?' said Ursula.

'Not everyone,' Sidney corrected. 'You didn't mention Eleanor Martinez.'

Julie snorted.

'No way. Flippin' oddball. She wouldn't be interested in that kind of thing. She's not a very sociable woman.'

'Was she invited to join?' Sidney asked.

'I don't really know,' Julie replied. 'The first time we set it up was after a barbecue at Bertie and Cissy's farm. Everyone in the close was invited because we were all new neighbours wanting to get to know each other. But Eleanor didn't attend.'

'Any reason for her not being there?' said Ursula.

Julie shrugged.

'Can't say for certain,' she said. 'Cissy mentioned to me a few days afterwards that there were some people that Eleanor probably didn't want to mix with. I don't know who she was referring to. Eleanor keeps herself to herself, if you know what I mean.'

Sidney recalled his conversation with Eleanor in her home. She did appear to be a shy and private kind of woman. Lonely, too, as shy people often are.

Ursula turned their attention back to the lottery. 'If you did win, how much money are we talking about?' she asked.

'If it was the weekend draw immediately before Fiona scarpered, and we had six numbers and the bonus ball, considering it was a rollover week with only one winning ticket, then it could be twenty-three million quid.'

Chapter 21

Seated in the restaurant of the Armada Hotel, Ursula noticed for the first time the prevailing theme in the decor of the room. It was quite a dimly lit space, owing to the dark oak panelling, low-beamed ceiling and small windows. But she noticed the pictures on the walls, each one illuminated by its own strip light. Most of the images were of seascapes, including one of the Giant's Causeway, another depicting the rope bridge at Carrick-a-Rede and several with an old sailing ship battling a raging sea. Ursula assumed this was yet another nod to the Spanish Armada and the *Girona*.

Sidney was quiet as he ate lasagne and drank wine, but Ursula was impatient to hear her father's thoughts on the case. Of course, her resultant babbling only served to irritate him.

'If we assume that there were nine members in the syndicate,' Ursula said, 'then that means they get roughly two and a half million each.'

'Not if they can't prove that they're entitled to a share,' said Sidney.

'What do you mean?'

Now resigned to having a conversation, Sidney put down his knife and fork.

'You hear of it happening all the time,' he said. 'People believe they are members of a lottery syndicate, but there's nothing formal in writing. The person in charge of making the entries can claim that a winning ticket is theirs alone, especially when the others have no knowledge of the numbers that were chosen.'

'So, one person can simply say that the winning line was their personal entry and was not a line owned by the syndicate?'

'Exactly.'

'You think that's what's happened with Fiona?' Ursula asked.

'Quite possible. Fiona could have placed multiple entries for each draw. She may have intended that some lines belonged to the syndicate while others could have been her personal entry. When the right numbers come up, she decides that all the money is hers regardless of whose line is whose. The others in the syndicate don't like it, obviously, and Fiona clears off.'

Ursula had a puzzled expression.

'That doesn't explain the murder of Teddy McNaughten,' she said. 'Or why he was dressed as a pirate.'

'I would imagine that twenty-three million quid would entice anyone to commit murder.'

'Well, first we need to confirm that there was a lottery win. That crowd in Finn Close might be getting in a tizz over naff all.'

'Eat your dinner,' Sidney scolded.

Without a word, Ursula bolted from the table and hurried out of the restaurant. Sidney shook his head, but at least he now had peace and quiet to finish his meal and to continue thinking. But the luxury didn't last for long. Two minutes later, Ursula returned, sat down with a smile and placed a small piece of paper before her father.

'That's the wee note I found in Teddy's bedroom.'

Sidney examined the slip of paper.

'So, you think these are the winning lottery numbers?' he said.

'I don't know, Daddy. It was you who suggested they could be lottery numbers in the first place.'

'I didn't really think they were important, but I suppose we can check them against the recent draws, see if they are winners.'

It took only a few minutes for Ursula to check the numbers on Teddy's note with recent lottery draws. In the meantime, Sidney was able to finish his dinner without further interruption. He was perusing the menu for dessert when Ursula again broke the silence.

'Seems that poor old Teddy won a tenner three weeks ago with one set of these numbers. That's if they were intended for the lottery. I had to group them as if they were, but it was a bit random.'

'And the rest?'

Ursula shook her head.

'Zilch. If the folks from Finn Close had a big win, it wasn't with these numbers. Then again, as we first thought, they might not be lottery numbers at all. Could be bank accounts. Maybe Swiss banks or secret accounts in the Cayman Islands.'

Sidney grimaced at Ursula's excitement.

'Let's leave the lottery win and the offshore accounts for now. It's not helping us to find Fiona McCabe.'

A waitress took their order for dessert. When she had left, Ursula spoke quietly to her father.

'Do you think that the body found on the Causeway will be identified as Fiona?'

'I'm trying not to think that, Ursula. If it is, I would have thought Eve would have been contacted by the police by now.'

'Maybe she already has but hasn't bothered to tell us.'

'I don't think so. If it is Fiona's body they've found, then Eve would no longer be requiring our services.'

When they had finished dinner, Sidney and Ursula wandered into the hotel bar. The room was bubbling with lively chat and laughter. A party of six fishermen were ensconced in a corner booth, teasing each other over a recent angling experience. A group of ramblers were chatting less noisily in another booth. That left three couples seated at separate tables and a group of young lads holding up the bar, laughing and taking selfies. It was lively for a country hotel midweek. Ursula instructed Sidney to find a table, while she went to the bar to get the drinks. She ordered a whiskey for Sidney and a white wine for herself from the barmaid. As she waited, one of the ramblers with a Welsh accent asked the barmaid if she knew whether the Causeway had reopened.

'Aye, I think so,' said the slim young woman. 'The police are finished, as far as I know.'

'What happened down there?' the man asked casually.

Ursula guessed he was in his sixties, retired perhaps. He smiled at her.

'A woman's body was washed up,' said the barmaid. 'The police believe she was murdered.'

'Is that so?' the man said. 'Terrible.' He lifted two pints of lager from the bar and carried them to his table. Ursula could hear him relate the news to his companions.

'Any idea what happened?' she asked the barmaid.

The woman set the whiskey on the bar and poured the wine. 'I heard the body was washed up on the rocks, but it doesn't seem like she drowned.'

'Oh?'

'There was a sword in her back.'

'How did you hear about that?' Ursula asked.

The barmaid leaned towards Ursula and looked around to check that no one else was listening. This was Northern Ireland and from time to time, old habits of not sharing police information died hard.

'My brother is a policeman. He was down there when they recovered the body.'

'Any idea who it is?'

'Did you not hear?'

Ursula shook her head.

'Sure, it was Natalie MacDonnell, pretty wee thing, lived up the road a mile or two. Used to be married to Harry MacDonnell, you know, MacDonnell's big hardware shop in Coleraine?'

'I don't, actually,' Ursula replied.

'He is a nasty piece of work, though, a drinker and gambler. Made poor Natalie's life a misery, beating her up and womanising. She was well rid of him.'

'Do you think he killed her?'

'I doubt it. They divorced years ago. If he was going to kill her, you'd think he would have done it long before now. Anyway, enough of this morbid talk. Have a nice evening.'

She set the wine on the bar and charged both drinks to Sidney's room.

Ursula could hardly contain herself on the way to join her father.

Chapter 22

On this occasion, Sidney managed to get a reply on his first attempt at calling Eve. He thought he should put her mind at rest over worrying that the body found on the Causeway was Fiona. Eve was grateful and relieved by the news but still worried about where Fiona had gone. Sidney took the opportunity to ask a few questions about the alleged lottery win. He imagined he could see Eve shaking her head in denial.

'I don't know anything about the lottery, Mr Valentine.'

'It's just that your name was also mentioned as being a member of the syndicate,' Sidney explained.

'Fiona never said anything to me about her doing the lottery.'

Sidney paused. He didn't wish to sound frustrated, but he couldn't shake the feeling that Eve was holding something back.

'What do you think has happened to your sister?' he asked.

'I really don't know. You hear so many stories nowadays about people getting a bump on the head, losing their memory, and not knowing who or where they are.'

Eve could be right but, considering their experience on the north coast, her theory wasn't helping.

'Did Fiona ever mention the wreck of the *Girona*?'

Ursula looked up from browsing her phone.

'I don't know what that is, Mr Valentine,' said Eve.

'One last thing, do you have a key to Fiona's house?'

'No, I'm afraid not. Although one of her neighbours might.'

'OK, I'll ask around,' said Sidney, trying not to sound disappointed. 'If you think of anything, give me a call.'

He sighed wearily as he ended his conversation.

'Why do I still think that woman is lying to us?' he said.

'It's her money, Daddy.'

'That would be fine if it were only a case of a missing person, but two people, Fiona's boss and one of her neighbours, have been murdered. A lie gets halfway round the world before the truth has a chance to get its pants on.'

'What?'

'Winston Churchill said that,' explained Sidney.

'I'm sure you're right. I only know the bit about fighting on the beaches. So, what are we planning to do tomorrow?'

'We're going to have a look inside Fiona's house.'

* * *

Next morning after breakfast, they drove to Finn Close yet failed to locate a spare key to Fiona's home from any of the neighbours they spoke to. Father and daughter, with a plan B in mind, moseyed to the rear of number two. Sidney held a small hammer in his hand and wasted no time in smashing a quarter pane of the kitchen window. The noise of shattering glass seemed to reverberate around them, disturbing the silence of the cul-de-sac. Sidney tapped the remaining shards of glass out of the frame, reached in and released the catch of the window in the same manner as he'd done at Teddy's cottage.

'In you go,' he said.

'How did I guess it would be me?' said Ursula.

'Dirt before the broom.'

'Delightful parenting. I should report you to Childline.'

'Give over and do as you're bid.'

Sidney gave his daughter a boost up, and she clambered through the space then dropped to the kitchen floor. A few seconds later, she opened the back door and Sidney joined her inside.

The air within the house was chilled and stale. Evidently, the place had not been heated for days. Sidney ventured immediately to the lounge, while Ursula began her search in the kitchen. The room was a shambles – drawers and cupboards had been left open, the contents scattered over the worktops. The chaos might well have been caused by Fiona, but it hadn't looked like this on Ursula's previous visit when she'd merely peered through the window. Ursula quickly lost interest and joined her father in the lounge. She found him seated comfortably in an armchair, browsing through a folder of what appeared to be personal correspondence. Letters, books and newspapers were strewn across the carpeted floor and sofa cushions had been pulled out of place. But Ursula's attention was captured by the picture on the wall above the sofa.

'Not another one,' she said with a groan. 'I'm beginning to think there's a *Girona* appreciation society based in this street.'

She was staring at the same image of the ship that she'd first noticed at Teddy's cottage. Sidney's interest, however, was centred upon the papers in his lap.

'It seems like our Fiona had a few financial problems. There are several unpaid credit card bills and a final warning from her building society. She hasn't been paying her mortgage.'

'A wee lottery win would have been very welcome then.'

Ursula's comment induced a bout of searching for anything related to the National Lottery – old tickets, lists of numbers or entry sheets – but she found nothing. She left Sidney engrossed in his reading and ventured to a bedroom.

The dishevelled room before her suggested a hasty departure from the house. Clothes were scattered around, the bed was unmade and an open suitcase lay on top of it. A couple of drawers from the dressing table had been pulled out. One had been cleared of its contents, the other had underwear hanging over the sides. Shoes littered the floor, and a wardrobe door lay open, revealing a row of empty coat hangers. Then she spotted a mobile phone on the bedside table. She tried to switch it on, but there was no charge left in the battery. Slipping it into the back pocket of her jeans, she continued her inspection of the room but found nothing to indicate why Fiona had departed or where she had gone. They still had no proof that the woman had won a fortune on the lottery. Again, the room had not been in this state on Ursula's first visit when she'd looked through the window. It seemed likely that Fiona had returned here at some point between then and now. But if she had fled her home once, why come back? Maybe someone else had ransacked the house.

Ursula had a cursory look in the other bedroom and the bathroom, but aside from several toiletry items abandoned by the washbasin, she found nothing to help explain Fiona's disappearance.

Rejoining Sidney in the lounge, Ursula was about to produce the phone she'd found when she noticed activity outside.

'Looks like we have company,' she sang.

'Not again,' Sidney groaned.

He rose from the armchair and gazed through the window. DI Kelso was standing, hands on hips, in the driveway of number four, the home of Natalie MacDonnell. Two uniformed officers were at the front door of the house attempting, it seemed, to force the lock.

'Damn,' said Sidney. 'I was hoping to get a look inside Natalie's house before the goon squad got here.'

Before Sidney could get out of sight of the detective, it was obvious that Kelso had spied him at the window.

'Oh dear,' he said. 'We're busted again.'

Chapter 23

'Seems you people can't keep your noses out,' DI Kelso said with a snarl. She'd confronted Sidney and Ursula after she'd beckoned them out of Fiona's house.

'I don't know what you mean, Inspector,' Sidney replied in his best sickly-sweet tone.

'I told the pair of you to go home and yet here you are interfering again with my investigation.'

'And how exactly are we interfering?'

'You're here, Mr Valentine, and that's more than enough interference for me.'

'We've been asked to check on Fiona McCabe's house by her sister. I can't see how that interferes with whatever it is you're doing.'

Ursula couldn't help smirking when she noticed the nervous tic erupt on Kelso's face.

The detective glared at Sidney but momentarily seemed lost for words. She shook her head in disgust.

'Just stay out of my way,' she mumbled.

'Quick question, Inspector,' said Sidney.

The detective had already begun to walk away, but she spun around with the scowl still on her face. 'What is it?'

'Can you confirm that Natalie MacDonnell is the person you found on the Causeway, and that she was murdered?'

'That's two questions, Mr Valentine.'

Sidney shrugged and grinned.

'Yes, OK, Natalie MacDonnell has been murdered,' Kelso replied.

'I heard she was killed by a sword,' said Ursula.

Kelso's face reddened. 'Where on earth did you hear that?' she said.

'The story is all over Bushmills,' Ursula replied. 'So, is it true?'

The police detective didn't look as though she could stand much more.

She puffed a sigh. 'Yes, a sword was used as the murder weapon. And if you have any information regarding this incident, I strongly advise you to tell us.'

'Anything special about the sword?' Ursula continued.

'What do you mean, special?'

'Was it modern or like an antique?'

Kelso walked off, shaking her head.

'Just interested,' Ursula called after her.

'Antique. Now please go home,' was Kelso's response.

* * *

Ursula bought sandwiches, crisps and fizzy drinks from a Spar in Bushmills then drove to Salmon Rock Beach at Portballintrae. This was a rather sedate, upmarket village just over a mile from Bushmills. Many of the white bungalows and holiday homes overlooked the sheltered cove, with the Bayview Hotel standing by the seafront. Salmon Rock Beach lay at the eastern headland of the cove. It was sunny but cool, so they remained in the van to eat their lunch and admire the view. They could see beyond the Girona Memorial across the bay to Runkerry House, a Victorian manor standing magnificently on the headland. While they ate, Ursula searched for a glazing firm they could hire to repair the damaged window at Fiona's house.

'Do you think DI Kelso is considering a link between the missing Fiona and the two murders?' she asked.

'Hard to know exactly what that woman is thinking. She's probably under pressure to get a quick solution to the mystery. Murders are never good for the tourist trade, especially in Northern Ireland.'

'She certainly doesn't appreciate us hanging around. What worries me is that there could be a third victim.'

'How do you mean?'

'Well, if Teddy and Natalie's murders are linked to Fiona, she could be the third victim. It's just that her body hasn't turned up yet.'

'Or she could be the perpetrator,' said Sidney.

'But why? If she's absconded with lottery winnings, what reason could she have for killing two people?'

'Maybe they were the people who most tried to prevent her from leaving.'

'I suppose, but we still need to establish if there was a big win on the lottery.'

'What about that phone you found in her house?' Sidney asked. 'You were going to show it to me when Kelso turned up.'

'Forgot all about it. I'll put it on to charge and we can check it later.'

Chapter 24

Sidney had just performed further handiwork with his hammer. This time, it was the kitchen window of number four, Finn Close, the home of Natalie MacDonnell. The police had already re-secured the front door after smashing their way in that morning. Sidney waited as Ursula clambered inside and released the lock on the back door. She was becoming quite the expert at entering houses by the kitchen window. Before Sidney could get inside, however, Cissy from next door appeared in her garden to retrieve some washing from her line. Over a low fence, she fired him a suspicious look then seemed to carry on as if nothing was wrong.

'Afternoon, Mr Valentine, it's a pleasant day,' she called.

'It is, indeed, Cissy,' Sidney replied, standing by the broken window. 'I'm sure you're wondering what we're up to?'

Cissy continued to gather her washing but said nothing. She seemed confident that more information would be forthcoming without having to dig.

'It's just that we're thinking it a bit strange, with all that's been going on, that no one wondered why Natalie's car was left in the drive.'

'I had noticed,' Cissy replied. 'The police pulled two suitcases out of the boot this morning.'

'You didn't suspect anything was wrong?' said Sidney.

'Natalie did what Natalie did, Mr Valentine. Neither you nor I were her keeper.'

Sidney was puzzled by her indifferent remark.

'How well did you know Natalie?' he asked.

At last, Cissy stopped what she was doing and approached the garden fence.

'I really only knew her by reputation. I would not have had much in common with young Natalie. She came and went. I didn't get involved, if you know what I mean.'

'I'm afraid I don't, Cissy. Was Natalie associated with something that you don't approve of?'

The woman's right shoulder gave an involuntary twitch as if the chip upon it was giving discomfort. Sidney guessed she was a woman who got much of her information from gossip and then jumped to assumptions accordingly.

'She was a divorced woman, Mr Valentine, and for a start, I do not approve of divorce. People should marry for life. That's what the Bible teaches.'

'I hear it was a rather abusive marriage, though.'

'That's as may be, but if you ask me, it takes two to tango. Natalie had a string of male companions since she moved here. Some of them were not what you and I would call respectable. And many of them stayed overnight. Natalie would wave them goodbye in the morning with hardly a stitch on her.'

'So, you didn't get on with Natalie?'

There was another shrug. Sidney reckoned he'd touched a nerve in the woman and now he was wiggling it about, producing further anguish.

'Natalie and I were perfectly fine, Mr Valentine. She was simply not the type of person I would regard as my friend.'

'Enough said, Cissy.'

'Good luck with whatever it is you're doing.'

The woman went inside and closed her door. Sidney had no doubt that she would watch his every move in future. He wondered if she was the secretary of the local knit and natter club. Narrow-minded people always left him bemused.

Ursula opened the back door, and Sidney was relieved to step inside. He could still feel the old woman's gaze upon him.

They performed a similar search of Natalie's home as they had done at Fiona's earlier in the day. It was obvious that this occupant had also made a hasty exit. The entire house was in disarray. Shoes and clothing, including some rather fetching lingerie and long boots, were scattered around the bedroom and hallway.

'Do you think the peelers made this mess?' Ursula asked, stepping around a pile of clothes on the lounge floor.

'I doubt it,' Sidney replied. 'After all, Natalie is a murder victim. Why would the police need to ransack the place? I would think DI Kelso would have wanted to get a feel for the victim and perhaps gather evidence when she called here and not turn the house upside down.'

'Did you notice something?' said Ursula, scanning the lounge walls.

'What?'

'There are no pictures of old sailing ships. No books on the subject either. Jilly Cooper and EL James seem to rule the roost here.'

'Never mind the books.'

Ursula looked at her father. He was holding a small notepad and frowning.

'What have you got?'

'Looks like Natalie had been planning a trip.' Sidney handed the notepad to Ursula.

'Flight times and a booking reference,' she said. 'We can check out the flight and the airport.'

'Won't help us much. Wherever Natalie was headed, she obviously didn't make it.'

'But it seems she had been trying to escape from something.'

Ursula had turned the page, and now was staring at a series of numbers.

'I wonder if these were intended as a lottery entry. There are four rows of figures,' she said. She flopped into a sofa and proceeded to check them with the National Lottery website.

'Do you know what I'm thinking?' said Sidney.

'That would take a special power, Daddy. Why don't you just tell me.'

'I'm thinking that I'm right. If this lottery-win story is true then Natalie and Teddy had challenged Fiona over it, and she's killed them both then scarpered.'

'I wonder where she got her hands on the fancy dagger that was stuck in Teddy's chest and the old sword used to kill Natalie.' Ursula got to her feet. 'Well, these aren't winning numbers. They don't even fit the pattern of six numbers plus a bonus. They could be anything.'

'Do you think the other neighbours already know the murders are linked to the lottery and that's why they've been cagey about sharing information? It's a conspiracy within the syndicate.'

'Then why did Julie even mention it?' said Ursula. 'Let's get out of here. This house is giving me the creeps, and I don't think we're going to find anything important.

Besides, we need to have a look at that phone I took from Fiona's house.'

* * *

Ursula spent her afternoon sprawled across her bed at the Armada Hotel, while Sidney went to his room for a nap. Once charged, it was surprisingly easy to gain access to Fiona's phone. The woman had not applied any security-controlled access. Ursula found text messages within a WhatsApp group called 'Lucky Us' and they were making interesting reading. It seemed that Fiona had been in contact with some of her neighbours in Finn Close in the week prior to her disappearance. Several of the exchanges concerned recent lottery draws. Four weeks ago, Cissy had asked how the previous night's draw had gone for them. Fiona had replied with a blunt 'nothing this week'. A week later, Curtis had requested a note of the numbers for the forthcoming draw, stating that it was a rollover week and he and Julie would like to check their numbers as the live draw was made. Fiona replied that she hadn't yet placed the entry but would get to it before the weekend. Natalie had texted once with the same question that Cissy had asked. Fiona did not reply. She had texted Eugene several times to remind him that he owed her money for recent lottery entries, to which he did not respond.

Next, Ursula read an exchange of texts between Teddy and Fiona. These concerned working arrangements for the Causeway tour business. In one message, Teddy explained that he was intending to visit the Ulster Museum in Belfast for a meeting about the treasure.

> Fiona: *Lol, not that again. I can do your Wednesday morning tour.*

> Teddy: *Thanks, pet. I'm getting closer to finding it. I'll buy you a pint when I'm stinking rich.*

Fiona replied with a tears-of-laughter emoji. Teddy's final message was to inform Fiona that Gary would cover the Wednesday afternoon tour.

Teddy's proposed meeting in Belfast set Ursula wondering. Had it taken place? And why had Teddy believed that he was getting closer to finding treasure?

She read strings of texts between Fiona and Eve, but there was nothing sinister about the rather stinted chat between sisters. One older message from Eve referred to a lottery draw, saying that she was chuffed to win a share of a tenner. She could buy herself a coffee in town. To Ursula, it confirmed that yet again Eve had lied to them when they had asked her if she knew about her sister's lottery syndicate.

One recent yet brief exchange of SMS texts involved an unidentified number on Fiona's phone. Ursula quickly browsed Fiona's list of recent numbers. It had appeared only once. The exchange raised more questions and answered none. Ursula read it again.

> *I know exactly what you're up to. I won't let you get away with it.*

Fiona's reply had been concise.

> *Leave me alone, bitch.*

Ursula called the number. It went straight to an automated voicemail.

She left a message, stating her name and business, but she didn't expect to receive a call back.

Chapter 25

Sidney, refreshed from his nap, had a sudden urge to solve the mystery immediately. Ursula helped him along by telling him what she had discovered on Fiona's mobile phone, including Teddy's intended meeting at the Ulster Museum.

'Somebody had also threatened Fiona,' she explained as they sat in the hotel bar.

'Do you know who it was?'

'No, but—'

'Find any emails from the lottery about Fiona winning the jackpot?'

'No, but—'

'Until we can prove that Fiona and her syndicate actually won a fortune then we're getting nowhere.'

'All right, smarty pants, then you tell me what we're going to do next.'

Sidney took a sip of his beer and sat back with a look reminiscent of the school swot, the only one in the class who'd solved the difficult maths equation.

'I've been thinking about Teddy,' he said. 'Why was he dressed as a pirate and why was he stabbed with what looked like a ceremonial dagger?'

'Good questions,' said Ursula, 'but we're no closer to answering them than we are to solving the lottery issue.'

'I think we might be. You see, I don't think Teddy was dressed as a pirate.'

'You don't? Frilly shirt, leather waistcoat, pantaloons and swashbuckling boots? Surely, he didn't walk around dressed like that every day.'

'Teddy wasn't dressed as a pirate,' Sidney explained. 'He was dressed as a Spanish nobleman from the time of the Armada. He was wearing clothes similar to what an officer on the *Girona* might have worn.'

'That doesn't tell us anything,' said Ursula. 'Unless he dressed in character when he was conducting his history tours?'

'And he was stabbed with a fancy-looking dagger,' Sidney mused. 'Is it possible that the weapon is connected with the treasure Teddy was searching for?'

'Jeepers, Daddy, I think we have more chance with the lottery angle. Who do you think would have killed him if it has something to do with his treasure hunt? And what about Natalie? None of this explains what happened to her.'

'Except for one thing. Natalie was killed with a sword, an antique sword according to DI Kelso. The modus operandi is similar for both killings. I think somebody knew that Teddy was getting closer to finding the *Girona* treasure and was prepared to kill to stop him.'

'And what about Natalie?' Ursula asked.

Sidney was less confident in his reply.

'Well, maybe she witnessed something and had to be gotten out of the way.'

Ursula suddenly rose from her seat and went to the bar as Sidney looked on bewildered. She returned a while later with fresh drinks and a rather satisfied smirk on her face.

'What's going on?' Sidney asked. 'You seemed to be having a deep discussion with the barmaid.'

'I was,' said Ursula. 'Her name is Karen. I was chatting with her the other night, remember? Her brother is a peeler, and he was at the Causeway when Natalie's body was discovered. She very kindly called him, and, through Karen, I asked him a couple of questions. The police reckon that the sword used to kill Natalie was quite tarnished and possibly hundreds of years old. It's been sent off for expert analysis. But here's the really interesting bit, Natalie was also dressed in a peculiar fashion when she was found.'

'What do you mean?'

'Well, she was wearing a costume that the police describe as being like something Madonna would wear on stage.'

Ursula grinned, watching Sidney trying to establish an image of the pop superstar in his head. She put him out of his misery by showing him a picture on her phone.

'The main feature is the cone-shaped bra,' she explained with a giggle. 'Apparently, that's what caught the attention of the cops.'

'I'm sure it did, but what does that tell us?' said Sidney, his brow furrowed.

Ursula smiled at her father's innocence.

'That maybe Teddy and Natalie were into dressing up?' she said.

Sidney didn't seem enlightened. He shrugged.

'You mean they were going to a fancy-dress party?' he said.

'Together, Daddy! They dressed up for each other. Role play, a prelude to having sex!'

'They were lovers?'

'Ker-ching! The penny drops.'

Chapter 26

Ursula left Sidney at Coleraine station in time for the 8.19 train to Belfast. He wanted to get more information about the sinking of the *Girona* and to view the collection of artefacts on display at the Ulster Museum. Sidney was hoping also to track down anyone at the museum who may have been in contact with Teddy regarding his search for *Girona* treasure. Perhaps they could help to establish if the tour guide's quest had been a viable endeavour. More importantly, what had they discussed when Teddy had visited the museum just days before he was murdered?

Less definite tasks lay ahead for Ursula. Since the trust level for any of the residents of Finn Close remained at zero, father and daughter had decided that as far as possible, they should establish what these people got up to each day. Was it possible that one or more of the residents knew the whereabouts of Fiona and were in regular contact with her? This surveillance was to be carried out, of course, without anyone suspecting they were being followed around.

There were six residents to be observed. The task was hardly straightforward, but Ursula began with Eleanor Martinez. As she waited in the lane by the entrance to Finn Close, Eleanor was the first person she saw leaving. Since it was a weekday, Ursula assumed that she was off to teach at the high school in Coleraine. It wasn't difficult to maintain a discrete distance behind the woman's Toyota on the ten-mile drive. Eleanor appeared to be a relaxed and cautious driver. Ursula watched from outside the school gates as the teacher entered the grounds and parked her car. When the woman strolled to the school building, Ursula drove away. She intended to catch up with Eleanor when she had left work at the end of the day.

She returned immediately to the lane off Causeway Road with a clear view of the vehicles in the close. It seemed that no one else had departed during the time she'd been following Eleanor. Only a few minutes elapsed until, as she browsed BBC News on her phone, a car emerged from the close and sped away. It was the customized Volkswagen Golf from number one, but she was unable to see whether it was Curtis or Julie behind the wheel, or even if both were inside. Quickly, she gunned her engine and followed. This was not going to be so easy as tailing Eleanor had been. Whoever was driving had little inclination to keep within the speed limit.

The Volkswagen, on reaching the junction with Causeway Road, turned left and headed towards Bushmills. Ursula lost sight of the car after it turned right onto Whitepark Road, but she assumed it was headed for the centre of town. Luckily, as she proceeded along Main Street, she glimpsed the vehicle turning right. She was about to follow when she noticed it had stopped just thirty yards further on. Aborting the turn, Ursula pulled over and watched as Curtis got out of the of the car driver's side. Julie emerged from the passenger side and the two of them kissed briefly. Curtis walked through a gateway, heading towards a building with a sign on the gable wall that read 'Dunluce Joinery Works'. Julie then got back into the car, drove to the bottom of what was a dead-end street, turned around and came back towards Ursula, who crouched in her seat as the Volkswagen entered Main Street and headed back the way it had come. Assuming Curtis had gone to work, Ursula decided it wiser to keep tabs on Julie.

It seemed that the young woman was now returning to Finn Close, and Ursula was less concerned about losing sight of her. As she reached the junction with the lane, however, Julie continued straight ahead. Ursula increased her speed to catch up and hoped she had not been noticed.

A mile or so further on, and in open countryside, she watched as Julie turned left into a lane where several holiday cottages sat near the junction. Ursula stopped by the entrance in time to see Julie's car disappearing over a hill. She decided to follow but guessed that she was probably entering a dead-end track. Reaching the brow of the hill, she spied the Volkswagen two hundred yards below coming to a halt in a farmyard. There was no way she could get much closer without being noticed, she thought. The lane was narrow, bordered on both sides with barbed-wire fencing and with no obvious places to make a U-turn. She drove on, knowing she was getting too close to the farm and might be spotted. After a few yards, she came to the gated entrance of a field, where the lane was a little wider, and considered it her best opportunity to turn the van around. She was much closer to the farmyard and noticed Julie getting out of her car carrying a cool box. There were three of what appeared to be glamping pods in the style of gypsy caravans standing to the left of a tall barn. Julie went to the first pod, climbed the steps, unlocked the door and went inside. Ursula didn't have a chance to maintain her vigil. A huge tractor had driven from the yard and was rolling up the lane towards her.

She quickly managed to turn her van by the gate and hurried back the way she had come. Reaching the top of the hill, she jumped hard on the brakes. A black SUV moving towards her had also come to a sudden halt. With her engine still running, she waited, hoping that the driver would reverse to a spot where she could get past, but the vehicle didn't move. Glancing in her mirror, she saw that the tractor had pulled up behind.

Confused and growing concerned, Ursula got out of the van, waved at the driver of the SUV then turned and smiled at the man behind the wheel of the tractor. She opened her hands wide, appealing for a little understanding. Then the door of the SUV opened, and the driver stepped out.

'Hello there, missy. What business have ye way up here?'

Chapter 27

Sidney had a pleasant morning. Firstly, he enjoyed the train ride to Belfast followed by a coffee and fruit scone at a shop in the city centre. Refreshed, he dandered through the Botanic Gardens to reach the Ulster Museum. By the time he arrived, he was ready for another coffee and a tray bake before casting his eyes over the artefacts retrieved from the wreck of the galleass *Girona*.

The permanent exhibition of the Spanish Armada was located on the second floor of a building that combined old architecture with new. Sidney read a brief account of the Armada story and of the tragedies that had befallen more than twenty Spanish ships off the Irish coast in the wake of the failed attempt to invade England in 1588.

The *Girona* had been captained by Fabrizio Spinola of Genoa. However, at the time of her sinking, she was commanded by Don Alonso Martínez de Leiva, from one of Spain's noblest families. Having already survived the wreck of two other ships, the *Santa Maria Encoronada* and the *Duquesa Santa Ana*, he'd learned that the *Girona* was sheltering in Killybegs Harbour in Donegal. He travelled north with the remnants of the crews and infantry of the other two ships. The *Girona* had a crew of three hundred but as she left Killybegs, she was woefully overcrowded. When the ship was lost in stormy seas at Lacada Point, near the Giant's Causeway, it was estimated that out of thirteen hundred souls on board, only a handful survived, but de Leiva was not one of them. Talk about bad luck, thought Sidney.

The next part of the story, Sidney quickly realised, was perhaps what inspired Teddy's search for treasure.

He read about the local chieftain, Sorley Boy MacDonnell, who lived nearby at Dunluce Castle, who helped the few survivors, arranging for their passage to Scotland. It was said that MacDonnell also organised salvage missions to the scene of the wreck. Two hundred and sixty bodies of those who drowned were recovered, afforded a Catholic funeral and were believed to have been buried at St Cuthbert's churchyard near Dunluce. The parish church of St Cuthbert's, that survived until 1821, was said to have held a chest within the building that had originally belonged to the *Girona*.

Sidney spent a while looking at the items recovered from the sunken wreck by Belgian divers, led by Robert Sténuit, in 1968. Hundreds of gold and silver coins had been retrieved, as well as the remnants of silver-gilt tableware and candlesticks designed to grace the table of the ship's aristocratic officers. The Spanish noblemen on board would have dressed in the same splendour as when they had attended the Spanish Royal Court of Philip II. Gold buttons and chains, orders of chivalry and glittering diamond rings were also recovered. Sidney recalled what Teddy McNaughten had been wearing when they'd found him murdered. Judging by the illustrations of Spanish nobles in the exhibition, Teddy had made a fairly accurate attempt to recreate the look.

The reasons why there was such wealth on board the *Girona* intrigued Sidney. The ship had been carrying officers of two other ships as well as the leaders of the Armada. Such men had been chosen from the noblest and wealthiest families in Spain. Philip II had also considered the Armada to be a religious crusade – its objective being to liberate England from Protestant domination under Elizabeth I. To support this venture, forty Roman Catholic clerics had also travelled on the ship.

Sidney stared through the glass display cabinet at the portrait cameos of Byzantine Caesars, in lapis lazuli, gold, enamel and pearls. These cameos would have been held within an ornate chain and worn by one of the *Girona*'s officers. Eleven cameos were recovered during the original exploration of the wreck, but it was suggested that there should have been a twelfth to complete the set. In 1997, almost thirty years after the first exploration of the wreck, a local diver discovered it. Two other unique jewels, a gold salamander set with rubies, and a gold ring with a salamander, or winged lizard, on the bezel, drew Sidney's interest. These items reflected the grandeur of the Spanish empire at the time of the Armada. In legend, a salamander was believed to have the magical ability to extinguish and survive fire. It was regarded as a good luck charm on board a wooden fighting ship, where fire was one of the greatest hazards. A pity it hadn't protected against a ship filling with water, thought Sidney. The hoard of gold and silver coins represented the personal wealth of those on board the ship. If there was a possibility of further treasures in existence, then Sidney could understand why Teddy had been so intent upon finding them.

Suitably empowered by a little knowledge of the *Girona's* history, Sidney wandered off in search of a person who may have been in contact with Teddy McNaughten. He didn't expect to find anyone merely standing around in the exhibition hall, so he went to the information desk on the ground floor and asked questions there.

It took nearly thirty minutes to locate a member of the collections team who came down to meet him. The young curly-haired man smiled cheerfully as he introduced himself but immediately announced that he was only a junior member of the team. When Sidney mentioned Teddy's name, however, the young man knew exactly who had been involved. He made a brief call on his phone, and after another ten minutes, a petite woman in her thirties, with cropped, fair hair and a friendly smile, introduced herself as Dr Arleen MacIntosh, deputy head of the collections department.

'I met Teddy recently,' she said, her accent lowland Scots. 'We also exchanged a few phone calls and several emails. How can I help you, Mr Valentine?'

Sidney told her of Teddy's murder and the connection with the missing Fiona McCabe. The woman was shocked by the news. Over coffee, Sidney asked her how seriously she regarded Teddy's quest for undiscovered *Girona* treasure.

'I thought he was a bit of a crackpot at first,' she said.

'But you changed your mind?'

'He was quite convincing. To be honest, Teddy had a greater knowledge of the *Girona* than I or any of my colleagues do. His experience of the Causeway coastline was impressive too.'

'Did he provide any hard evidence that there could be outstanding treasure from the *Girona*?'

Dr MacIntosh smiled at Sidney's question. He thought her quite an attractive woman. She had lively eyes and spoke with confidence.

'Perhaps treasure is too grand a word, Sidney,' she replied. 'Most of what we have on display was recovered from the wreck in the late 1960s. A few items have been found since then, all the result of further dives to the wreck. I'm not so sure there is much more to be found there.'

'But Teddy wasn't referring to recovery of items from the sunken wreck, was he? He was convinced that a hoard of valuables was brought ashore perhaps by the survivors on the night the ship went down or were recovered shortly afterwards. The ship was packed to the rafters with Spanish noblemen, all of whom had many valuables with them. I've just been reading about it.'

'But there were very few survivors,' Dr MacIntosh countered. 'It's hard to imagine how they could have managed to save themselves *and* their belongings.'

'Not impossible, though,' said Sidney. 'Or so Teddy believed. I read also about the chieftain who helped the survivors and arranged burial for some of the victims. Seems plausible that he may have got his hands on a few valuables from the wreck. It seemed that Teddy was convinced of it.'

'He referred to documentary evidence regarding the fate of the survivors,' said MacIntosh, 'how they were helped by locals in their attempts to make it home to Spain.'

'Surely that wasn't new to you either. What convinced you that Teddy was really onto something?'

Dr MacIntosh grinned at the question and looked to be considering her response.

She cleared her throat. 'Teddy had already found some items. He showed them to me. These were objects that, judging by their condition, had not spent four hundred years under the sea.'

'And these items definitely came from the *Girona*?'

'Yes, I believe so. We were hoping to arrange to have them verified, but I suppose with Teddy dead that won't be happening for a while.'

'What are we talking about here?' Sidney asked.

'Teddy showed me two pieces of religious jewellery, several coins, a sword and two ornate daggers.'

* * *

Sidney caught an early-evening train back to Coleraine, his mind still buzzing with what he'd learned at the museum. Dr MacIntosh's revelation about *Girona* treasure raised more questions. Had Teddy uncovered a vast collection of valuables from the Spanish ship? Or had he been on the trail of what he believed existed and had merely stumbled upon a few items? Maybe he'd found them using his metal detector. Had he been murdered because he'd uncovered a fortune? Or had someone killed him to stop him finding it? What had been Natalie's role? It seemed likely that both victims had been killed by the very weapons Teddy had shown to Dr MacIntosh.

Half an hour out from Coleraine, Sidney texted Ursula with his arrival time so that she could meet him at the station. There was no reply, but he imagined she was probably en route. When he walked out of the station building in Coleraine, however, there was no sign of Ursula or their van.

Chapter 28

Sidney tried calling Ursula, but her phone went immediately to voicemail. He left several messages, the last one stating that he would get a taxi back to the hotel in Bushmills. Eventually, he managed to find one that had just dropped a couple off at the station. When he reached the Armada Hotel, he asked at reception if they knew the whereabouts of his daughter. Neither of the two receptionists recalled seeing Ursula during the afternoon since they'd come on duty. Outside, he looked around the hotel's car park for their white Vauxhall van then gazed up and down Main Street, but there was no sign of it. What worried him most was that this was so unlike Ursula. She was always nagging him about staying in touch, especially when they were working. He checked his phone again, but there were no voicemails or replies to his texts. Next, he went up to her room and knocked on the door but got no answer. Returning to reception, he ordered another taxi.

Twenty minutes later, he was deposited in Finn Close, and the taxi driver waited while Sidney rang the doorbell of number five, the home of Cissy and Bertie. It was Cissy who opened the door.

'Mr Valentine, what brings you here?' she said with a weak smile.

Sidney got the feeling that the people in the close were growing weary of his enquiries. He quickly explained his concern that he was unable to find Ursula.

'I haven't seen your daughter about the close today. Maybe she's met a friend and they've been shopping, or they've gone out for dinner. Young people are inclined to do such things nowadays. Sometimes the parents are the last to know.'

Sidney winced. No way had Ursula simply met up with a friend. Besides, she would at least have answered her phone and was unlikely to have forgotten to pick him up at the station. Cissy offered nothing further and seemed eager that Sidney should be on his way. He thanked her and got back into the taxi. The woman remained on her doorstep watching until they drove away.

He couldn't think of anywhere else to look for Ursula, so he returned to the hotel and repeated his search of the car park and checked her room again. The remainder of his evening was spent sitting in the foyer of the hotel, glancing from his phone to the door. When it grew late, he went to his room and lay down on his bed. Sleep wouldn't come. His mind raced. He listened to the late-night bulletin on TV for any news of road accidents in the area but there was nothing. Everything pointed to this damn case. Two people murdered, a woman missing, a strange bunch of people linked to both and all living in the same street. He didn't like it.

Exhaustion finally got the upper hand and Sidney nodded off. He jumped awake at six in the morning, the TV still playing looped news items about floods in Indonesia and internet scams in the south of England. He checked his phone. Still nothing from Ursula. After a brief visit to the bathroom, he hurried out and knocked on her door but got no response. He went down to reception and asked the night porter if he had seen her. The middle-aged man was sympathetic but merely suggested that Sidney contact the police.

* * *

The old police station in Bushmills had closed years ago. Another taxi ferried him to the station in Coleraine. These were the days of supposedly modern policing and Sidney stood on the outside of a locked gate reading the sign that said the station opened to the public at eleven o'clock. That was nearly four hours he would have to wait.

After wandering the streets of Coleraine town centre for almost an hour, he at last found a café open and serving breakfast. There were two customers inside, both male and alone like him. A cheery woman with a loud voice took his order for coffee and a fry stack. Sidney didn't know if he would be able to eat anything when the food arrived but at least the coffee would revive him. He tried calling the police station but only got a recorded message with options for reporting crimes. For a moment, he considered leaving a message describing the most violent heinous incident he could imagine just to see if it provoked a response, but instead he cut the call and browsed through his last texts with Ursula. Maybe he would find a clue to where she might be. He hoped she was somewhere through choice and not because of the actions of others.

At eight o'clock he called the station again, but this time hung on until he got a human on the other end. A dull male voice asked how he could be of help.

'Can I speak to DI Kelso, please?'

Chapter 29

Ursula awoke after a surprisingly comfortable night. A soft bed with a fresh-smelling sheet and duvet helped. She couldn't say the same for the handcuffs securing her left wrist to the metal bed frame. She wondered what kind of people kept handcuffs just in case they needed to kidnap a woman who'd strayed into their world. Weak sunshine, breaching a gap in the curtains, illuminated the room. Ursula lay staring at a curved wood-strip ceiling and panelled walls, the furniture trimmed with pale-green chintz. All very rustic and very cosy except that she was a prisoner. As for who her hosts were, she had no clue, but her drowsiness didn't slow her speculation. They must, she thought, be in cahoots with the residents of Finn Close. She'd ended up in this pickle after following Julie down a farm lane. She'd watched her going into a glamping pod carrying what looked to be a cool box. One of those pods now seemed to be her prison.

The two men who had trapped her van in the lane as she tried to drive away were strangers. They were not Finn Close residents. The man in the SUV seemed to be in charge. He had said little more than to ask what she was doing on the lane, then stood grinning as his younger companion had jumped down from the tractor and snatched Ursula's phone from her hand as she tried to call Sidney. He'd shoved her towards the SUV where the older man was already holding the passenger door open for her. Ursula stopped. No way were these guys taking her. But the tractor boy grasped her upper arm, squeezed hard and propelled her forward.

'I wouldn't argue with our Royston, missy,' the older man had said. 'He always does what I tell him, ye see. One word from me and he'll rip that cute wee face from your head.'

'What do you want with me?' said Ursula. 'I made a wrong turn. I didn't mean to come this way.'

'Nice try. We'll talk about it at the house. Now get in. Royston needs his tea break.'

Fear pulsing through her, Ursula had climbed into the SUV and the man slammed the door. He jumped into the driver's side, started his engine and waited until Royston had opened the gate into the field and moved the tractor off the lane. Ursula watched as the burly youth then jumped into her van and reversed it out of the way. That left the lane clear, and the man roared the SUV downhill to the farmyard. They came to a halt close to the back door of the farmhouse, an old, grey-rendered building with sash windows with a modern kitchen extension. Ursula considered making a run for it, but as she threw open the door of the SUV and jumped out, Royston had already emerged from her van and stood waiting to greet her.

'What did you think of her?' she joked. 'The gears are a wee bit clunky, but she handles well.' She tried to sound cocky, but the youth merely glared.

'Royston doesn't say much,' said the farmer. 'He's hardly uttered a word in five years, ever since Jodie was run over by a muck spreader.'

'Jodie?'

'Aye, our sheepdog.'

Ursula smiled sympathetically at the youth with brown dishevelled hair and a navy boiler suit. His intense gaze remained fixed on her, but he avoided eye contact.

The farmer proceeded to the kitchen door, and Ursula was the recipient of another hefty shove from Royston.

'Easy on, Royston mate. It's not nice to push a girl, you know.'

That made him chuckle as he thrust his bulging stomach into her back, and she had little option but to follow the farmer into the house. As she stepped inside, she glanced behind her in time to see the Volkswagen rushing out of the yard and onto the lane. No chance then of Julie coming to her rescue.

The kitchen was spacious and echoed from the clatter of mugs being set upon a sturdy table in the middle of the room. A delft teapot, milk jug, sugar bowl and a plate of chocolate digestives were already upon it.

'Sit yourself down, missy,' the man said. It was more an order than invitation. 'You can at least have a wee sup of tea while you explain what you've been up to.'

Royston sniggered as he poured the tea into three blue-and-white-striped mugs. He sat down and immediately tucked into the biscuits. Ursula had little option but to sit next to his bulky frame. The farmer slid a mug of strong tea in front of her.

'Help yourself to milk and sugar. You'd better grab a biscuit before Royston scoffs them all.'

Another chuckle from Royston was stifled since his mouth was full.

'Are you going to tell me who you are and why you've abducted me?' she said.

The man laughed heartily, and Royston joined in.

'I think you should be telling us who you are and what you were doing on our lane,' said the farmer.

'I've told you. I took a wrong turn.'

The farmer's rosy cheeks coloured further in amusement. He had lively and friendly blue eyes. Ursula found it hard to believe he was up to no good. She realised he was still waiting for an answer to his question.

'I'm Ursula Valentine, SV Solutions,' she stated.

'And what pray tell is SV Solutions?'

'I work with my father Sidney Valentine. We're private detectives.'

The man drew a long breath.

'Boyso! Private detectives, eh? Like that bloke Endeavour off the television? And what would you be doing investigating the likes of us?'

'Endeavour is a cop in a period drama, not a private detective. Not important. Anyway, I am searching for a missing person, Fiona McCabe. Do you know anything about that?'

Ursula saw no trace of recognition on the man's face, but she glanced at Royston. He seemed to bristle at the question, but as she stared, he quickly stuffed another biscuit into his mouth.

'Well, Miss Ursula Valentine,' said the farmer in a peculiarly jolly tone, 'finish your tea. You'll be our guest until we can decide what to do with you.'

He rose from the table and rinsed his mug at the sink. Ursula's protestations came thick and fast.

'You can't stop me leaving! Who do you think you are? I'll get the police. You haven't even told me your name.'

'Calm yourself, missy. Drink your tea. No need for tantrums.'

Not another word had been said. Ursula sipped the rest of her tea as she waited for the farmer to explain what was going on. The next thing she was aware of was waking up and staring at the ceiling of a glamping pod, her left wrist handcuffed to the bed.

Chapter 30

'Do you know, in a certain light, you have a very pleasant face – very caring, I would say.'

'What exactly do you want, Mr Valentine?'

DI Kelso was standing, hands on hips, in the foyer of Coleraine police station. She didn't look pleased at being confronted so early in the day by a man who had been frequently getting on her goat. Sidney's feeble attempt to soften her up had crashed and burned.

'It's my daughter, Ursula. She's missing.'

Sidney detected little change in the DI's expression. Perhaps cold to icy, but there was no trace of concern or even mild interest.

'You seem to be losing people instead of finding them,' she said.

'She was supposed to pick me up at the railway station last night. When I got to Bushmills, she wasn't at our hotel.'

'Maybe she heeded my instruction and has gone home to Belfast.'

'Holywood.'

'Sorry?'

'We don't live in Belfast; we live in Holywood.'

'Whatever. You say you haven't seen her since yesterday, is that correct?'

'Yesterday morning when she left me at Coleraine station.'

'So, it's only been twenty-four hours. Have you any idea where she was going after she'd dropped you at the station?'

Sidney cleared his throat. He was reluctant to explain to this detective that Ursula had been intending to carry out surveillance on the residents of Finn Close.

'Not really,' he managed to reply.

'Have you had any contact with her?'

'There's been no answer to my calls.'

'Well, twenty-four hours for a grown woman to be out of contact with her family is not enough for us to act upon, Mr Valentine. I suggest you keep trying to reach her. Maybe try calling her friends. And as I said before, go home to Belfast. You might find that she's already there.'

'Holywood,' Sidney grumbled.

The cop had disappeared through a doorway before Sidney could protest. He'd hoped to tell Kelso all about the strange goings-on at Finn Close and Teddy McNaughten's search for Spanish treasure. He knew it had to be linked to Ursula's disappearance, but that damned detective wasn't interested. He was just getting in the way of her investigation. He'd dearly love an update on how that was going. Two murders and two missing persons, and the peelers had no interest in what he had to say.

Sidney felt at a loss over what to do next. He had no daughter, no transport and no clue. He walked from the police station to a bus stop, and after waiting for half an hour, caught a bus to Bushmills. On the journey, he had an idea, but it was hardly an epiphany – he was on the road to Bushmills not Damascus – but at least it made him feel that he was doing something to find Ursula. Issues of a missing Fiona and two murders would have to wait. He hoped Ursula was OK, wherever she was.

When he got to the Armada Hotel, he went directly to the bar, hoping to find the person who might be able to help him. A young woman dressed in the hotel's staff uniform with her brown hair pinned up was placing bottles into a cooler behind the bar.

'Excuse me, Karen,' Sidney cheeped.

The woman turned around. 'What can I get you, sir?' she said.

'I just wanted to ask you a few questions.'

Sidney began by explaining who he was, but the woman just smiled.

'Oh, I know who you are, love. I was chatting with your daughter the other night. And besides, it's all over the hotel that you are private detectives.'

'Oh, right,' said Sidney with disappointed surprise. So much for covert surveillance, he thought. He got on with asking his questions.

'Ursula told me that your brother is a police officer?'

'Aye, he is indeed.'

'Has he mentioned what progress has been made with investigating the two murders?'

'Nothing specific,' said Karen.

Sidney nodded his understanding, but his sombre expression betrayed him.

'Is everything all right, Mr Valentine? I didn't see your daughter around yesterday.'

'That's the thing. She's disappeared. I can't find her anywhere.'

'Did you call the police? I could tell our Martin. He'd know what to do.'

'That would be very kind. I spoke to DI Kelso earlier, but she said it was too soon to be launching a search.'

'Typical Pamela.'

'What do you mean?'

Karen leaned closer and spoke quietly despite there being no one else in the bar.

'Pamela Kelso always does things her way and in her own time, no matter about anyone else.'

'You know her?'

Karen tittered. 'Oh yes. She used to be my Sunday school teacher. She behaved like she ran a private school for girls. We had to sit with our arms folded, back straight and woe betide you if you hadn't learnt our Bible verses each week. It was no surprise to me that she became a cop. Where else can she get to order people around? A real bully, is our Pamela.'

Based on his own experience of the police detective, Sidney couldn't dispute Karen's opinion. Since the barmaid seemed to be well tuned into the community, he asked what she knew of the folk in Finn Close.

'They're a mixed bunch,' she said, maintaining her whispered tone as if she were imparting state secrets. 'Poor Natalie, I'm sure you already know about her. Pamela Kelso hasn't said much about finding the killer, but as I said, she'll do things her way.'

'How well do you know Fiona McCabe?'

Karen shook her head. 'Not that well. I saw her in here a few times with Teddy and Gary, but I can't recall having a conversation with her. Eleanor is another strange fish, a bit like Pamela Kelso. She taught me history in fourth year at school. It's funny though, Eleanor, Pamela and Teddy all grew up together. They lived in the same road, went to the same school. Bushmills is a very small town, Sidney. Everybody knows everybody.'

'That postman fella seems a bit odd,' said Sidney.

'Eugene? He's very quiet and very shy.'

'Still waters run deep.'

'Ach, I think Eugene could do with a few close mates or maybe a night in bed with a good woman.' She laughed.

'A bit repressed, is he?'

'Ish.'

'What about the young couple, Curtis and Julie?'

'Can't say I know much about them. They're blow-ins, you see, not from round here. They come from Portrush.'

Sidney smiled at the parochial attitude. That someone from just six miles along the coast could be referred to as a blow-in.

'And that elderly couple?'

'Cissy and Bertie? Salt-of-the-earth kind of people,' said Karen in a brighter tone. 'Bertie handed over the running of the farm to his son, you know. He and Cissy own the land where Finn Close is built. When the houses were ready, they decided to have one for themselves. Can I get you a drink, Sidney?'

'It's a bit early for me, but a coffee would be nice.'

Karen turned to prepare the coffee machine but continued chatting. It appeared that she was very adept in that pursuit. Sidney thought her rather too young to be embroiled in so much gossip. To him it seemed more of a middle-aged thing.

'You're not thinking that somebody in Finn Close has anything to do with these murders, are you?' she said.

Before Sidney could reply, Karen jumped to her next speculative question.

'Oh my God, you don't think somebody up there has snatched your daughter?'

Sidney rubbed the side of his face and decided not to reveal all that he was thinking. He was still hoping that Karen's brother could provide an update on the police investigation.

'If Ursula has been abducted, then I'm thinking it is the same people who may have taken Fiona McCabe and quite possibly murdered Teddy and Natalie,' he said.

Karen set a coffee and some milk in front of Sidney. Her expression now seemed rather grave.

'Right then. I'll call our Martin. He should be off today, and you and him can have a wee chat.'

Chapter 31

Ursula was bored now. The bed didn't feel quite so comfortable, the wee hut not so cosy. The big farmer bloke with no name, who wore a smelly boiler suit and wellies, had brought her ham sandwiches and orange juice, but that seemed like hours ago. She couldn't decide if it were intended as breakfast or lunch. Without her phone, she had no idea of the time or how long she had been asleep. The farmer had said nothing while she fired a barrage of questions, protests and threats at him. To each remark he merely grinned then left her spitting teeth and shouting the place down. A while later, the habitually silent Royston came in. She bombarded the youth with the same diatribe, but since he hadn't uttered a word for years, she didn't expect a worthwhile response. And she was right. She got nothing. Instead, he paused by the door and stared rather intensely at her lying on the bed. He swiped a dirty hand across his mouth.

Staring at the young farmer, Ursula felt a rush of fear. Was he intending to exercise some captor's rights on his prisoner? He may not say much, but was Royston about to express his manliness in a sordid manner? He stepped towards her. Ursula reeled back on the bed as far as she was able. Her wrist was still held fast by the handcuffs.

'Get away from me!'

The big lad just grinned. Ursula screamed as loud as she could. She pressed herself into the corner of the bunk. Royston produced a roll of gaffer tape from the pocket of his boiler suit and leaned over her. Ursula rolled her head to resist but the lad was powerful. He secured the tape around her head and mouth before she could summon appropriate swear words to describe the beast. Royston stepped back and seemed to admire his handiwork. Ursula used her eyes to strike him down dead. Ineffectual, of course, but she had to do something in protest. She had been kicking up a racket and evidently, the farmer with no name had ordered his son to silence her. The final insult was Royston patting her playfully on the head. He grunted then backed away. She heard him locking the door then whistle as he walked away. He'd left her right hand free, and she began to peel the tape from her mouth.

As her heart rate slowly returned to normal, she wondered what Sidney was up to. She knew he would be doing his head in worrying about his wee girl. Then fear took over when she imagined that she might never be found. After all, they'd come to the north coast to find a missing woman and had got nowhere except become embroiled in the murders of two people. It seemed likely that everything was connected. This scary farmer had taken her prisoner and had likely done something similar with Fiona McCabe. Was it plausible that he and his gump son had also killed Teddy and Natalie? But why? Was it really all about winning the lottery? And surely this farmer wasn't a member of the Finn Close syndicate. She was struck by a harrowing thought. What if they had killed Fiona too and she was next?

She kicked her heels against the wall until they hurt. Free of the gaffer tape, she yelled as loud as she was able. She tried bouncing on the bed. If she ever got out of here, she would definitely post a review on TripAdvisor. These glamping pods were sturdily built. Five stars. As for friendliness of staff – a big fat zero.

When she had calmed down, once more her thoughts returned to the previous day. She had ventured into the farm lane because she had been following Julie. Why had she come to the farm? And why had she gone directly to one of these glamping pods?

Her thumping hadn't gone unheeded. Royston burst in holding a bunch of cable ties. When he leaned over to bind her feet, she kicked out and scored a direct hit on his left eye.

'Ow!'

'Well, it's nearly a word, Royston love,' she said. 'Will I give you another kick? Maybe get a whole sentence out of you.'

Royston glared. He didn't look happy. He bound Ursula's feet, and with another cable tie fastened her free hand to the bed frame. Then he renewed the gaffer tape around her mouth. She thought she heard him mutter something as he departed. Maybe it was just a grunt of satisfaction, but she hoped it was of discomfort. She was certain he'd have a black eye in the morning.

Chapter 32

Constable Martin Dawson looked quite athletic. He wore a green sweatshirt over a wide chest and jogging shorts that revealed muscular legs. He shook hands with Sidney when Karen introduced them and accepted the offer of a drink. Karen smiled when her older brother ordered nothing stronger than a pint of orange squash. There were no other customers, and the two men remained at the bar. Sidney imagined that Karen would be interested in hearing the conversation too.

'Karen tells me your daughter has gone missing,' said Dawson with a broad and lively north Antrim accent. It wasn't hard to picture this man as a uniformed police officer.

'And you've reported this to Pamela Kelso?' Dawson asked once Sidney had explained the situation.

'I have, but I don't think DI Kelso was taking me seriously. I seem to have irritated the woman.'

'That's not hard to do,' said Dawson. 'How do you think I can help you?'

'I've been linking Ursula's disappearance with Fiona McCabe's. And I'm working on the theory that Fiona going missing is connected to the murders of Teddy McNaughten and Natalie MacDonnell. I thought if you could give me an update on the murder investigation, it might help me to find Ursula.'

Martin Dawson winced. Sidney realised he was asking a lot of the police constable.

'We don't have much, to be honest,' he said. 'Unless DI Kelso isn't sharing and that wouldn't surprise me. She likes to keep stuff to herself but takes all the plaudits when a case has been cracked.'

'Please, tell me what you know; it might be more than I have so far,' said Sidney. 'For instance, have you identified any other suspects for the murders?'

'We are proceeding with the theory that Fiona McCabe is responsible. The killing of Teddy McNaughten suggests a female perpetrator. A knife was used. It was a surprise attack, no signs of struggle, no robbery, and Fiona knew the victim. And, of course, the woman has disappeared.'

'So, you believe that Fiona has made herself scarce, not that she's been murdered or abducted?'

Dawson nodded.

'What about Natalie?'

'We think Fiona McCabe killed her around the time she murdered Teddy. Natalie may have been an unfortunate witness. She perhaps saw Fiona fleeing Teddy's cottage.'

'Karen was telling me that Teddy, Eleanor Martinez and DI Kelso grew up together. How did Kelso react when she saw Teddy dead?'

'She didn't say much,' Dawson replied. 'Cold as usual, although I did see her wandering off into a field, supposedly to make a phone call, but when she rejoined us, she looked as though she'd been crying.'

'So, the woman does have a heart?'

'In a small town like Bushmills, people are still neighbourly, the way it was everywhere in the old days. I would think that Teddy, Pamela and Eleanor would have been fairly close when they were kids.'

'Or maybe they hated each other,' said Sidney.

The policeman didn't disagree. Sidney realised he wasn't about to receive any earth-shattering information from the constable, but he had one last question.

'If you're working on the idea that Fiona McCabe is the killer and that she has now fled the area, who do you think has taken Ursula?'

'Sorry, I have no idea, but if you give me some details about your daughter, a description and where she was going when you last saw her, I will raise a missing person report immediately, never mind what Kelso said.'

Sidney provided details of Ursula, and their van's registration. He thanked Martin Dawson and Karen for their help then went up to his room. He thought another chat with Eve was overdue.

It was no surprise when her phone switched immediately to voicemail. He left a message, conscious that he sounded angry and frustrated with his client. When he finished the call, he decided that as soon as he'd found Ursula, they would go home and forget all about this case.

* * *

Outside, it was a cool afternoon but thankfully dry. Sidney began walking along Main Street just to get some fresh air at first, then he realised that Finn Close wasn't too far away. He could make a nuisance of himself until someone in that street gave him answers. He was convinced that some of the residents knew something.

He walked briskly along Whitepark Road and when the pavement came to an end, stuck closely to the side, remaining vigilant for cars speeding by. At the Smugglers Inn, he joined Causeway Road and felt a little safer by walking on the grass verge. He spent the time going over recent events in his mind, trying to make sense of why someone had snatched Ursula. He knew her well enough to know that being abducted was the only explanation for her disappearance. Martin Dawson hadn't referred to a lottery win or a search for treasure from the Spanish Armada as a motive behind the murders. The police theory that Fiona McCabe was responsible rankled with him. If Fiona had scarpered after committing murder, why hadn't she at least contacted her sister Eve? According to Eve, the pair of them were close. Surely, Fiona would have needed help, if only to get further away. He felt his agitation rise. Somebody in Finn Close was going to have a bad night until he got answers.

Chapter 33

Ursula was freezing. Securely bound and gagged, she'd been unable to gather the duvet around her. The daylight was fading, and no one had come with food. All she could do was lie still and listen for activity outside. She thought again about seeing Julie going into one of these pods. Perhaps Fiona McCabe was also being held here, and Julie had been coming to check on her and maybe bring her food. But none of that made sense.

Drifting in and out of sleep, Ursula had imagined hearing cries and shouting but couldn't be certain they came from another pod. She wondered what Sidney was doing and knew he'd be sick with worry. Of course, he would blame himself for them getting involved in this debacle.

She heard footsteps outside on the gravel. A few seconds later, the door was unlocked, and it swung open. The farmer with no name filled the space.

'Well, missy, how are we doing?'

Ursula glared, her best attempt at defiance. Besides, she was in no position to reply.

'I've brought you some supper.'

He held a small tray with a plate of sausages and baked beans, buttered bread and a mug of strong tea.

'You have to promise me not to kick up a racket,' he said. 'If you do, then the tape stays on and you can figure out how to eat. Do you get me?'

Ursula said nothing, and the farmer took it as compliance. He set the tray on a small table fitted to the wall then removed the tape from her mouth and released her hands and feet.

'You're in big trouble when my daddy catches up with you,' she said, taking her first free breath for hours. It was all she could muster by way of threat.

'Is that so?'

'Is this how you treat everybody who makes a wrong turn in your lane?'

'Let's stop with the games, missy.'

'Games? You're the one playing games. Why are you keeping me here? What have you done with Fiona? And why did you kill Teddy and Natalie?'

'Woh! Hold on there, missy. You're getting way ahead of yourself, so ye are. Eat your supper; that's enough of your chatter.'

He stomped away, closing and locking the door as he went. Ursula had gained nothing from her questions. All she could do was accept his refusal to answer as admission of his guilt.

She rose from the bed and peered between the curtains over the tiny window. Her view was restricted to the neighbouring glamping pod, just eight feet away. She stared at its window, but the curtains were drawn. Was someone inside and had they been calling for help? If so, then surely it must be Fiona. Ursula couldn't make sense of anything. She recalled the farmer's words when he told her that she would be held until 'they' decided what to do with her. Who were 'they'? Was it merely the farmer with no name and big Royston? Or were the residents of Finn Close involved?

She sat on the edge of her bunk with the food tray on her lap and began to eat the meal of sausages and baked beans with a plastic knife and fork. She'd been lying down all day, gagged and bound, yet surprisingly she'd worked up an appetite. It occurred to her that the food or the tea might be drugged but she was ravenous and ate regardless. When she'd finished, she scoured the tiny room for something, anything that might help her to escape. But the pod held only fixings, furnishings and, mercifully, a chemical toilet placed in one corner. There were no loose implements that she could use to force the lock on the door. She inspected the window, but it didn't even have a latch. Smashing it wouldn't get her far, this time there was no way she could squeeze through the opening. Besides, the farmer with no name would hear the glass breaking.

Darkness had descended by the time she'd given up on the idea of escaping. There was no lighting or heating in the pod. A log burner had been installed, but there was no wood to go with it. Ursula lay down beneath the duvet, and soon she felt a little warmer. Sleep was approaching when, this time, she was certain that she heard someone screaming and it was coming from the next pod.

Chapter 34

The red door of house number three opened slightly. Sidney kicked it wide to the wall. Eugene staggered backwards.

'Clear off! I'll call the cops,' he shouted.

Sidney ignored the threat and stamped into the house, shoving the young man towards his living room.

'Somehow I don't believe you will,' Sidney said. 'You and I are going to have a wee talk, sunshine.'

'Who are you? What do you want from me?'

Eugene backed away from his visitor. He had a scrawny build and would be no match for a determined Sidney. Scrambling into his lounge, he glanced around for something to use as a weapon. Sidney clocked his intention and pounced before Eugene got his hand to the poker on the fireplace. The two men crashed to the laminate floor with Sidney on top.

'We can either continue like this,' said Sidney, 'or you can calm down and talk to me man to man.'

'OK,' Eugene groaned under Sidney's weight.

Cautiously, Sidney released his host and clambered to his feet. He watched as Eugene crawled onto his sofa. Sidney, with the poker in his hand, took to the only armchair in the room.

'What do you want with me?' Eugene said, his voice lacking confidence.

'You've already met my daughter, Ursula. She's gone missing, and I believe it's connected to what's been going on around here. So, you're going to tell me everything, or I promise you I will make good use of this poker. Do you understand me?'

Eugene folded his arms more out of fear than defiance.

'Understand?' Sidney repeated.

Scarcely raising his head, Eugene nodded once.

'Right. Off you go. Tell me what you're all up to.'

'I don't know what happened to Teddy or Natalie, I swear.'

'What about Fiona?'

Eugene began to shake his head. Sidney raised the poker.

'All right,' Eugene said, his hands open wide in surrender, 'but it's got nothing to do with me, honest.'

'Start talking, sunshine, or so help me I'll mash what brains you have with this thing.'

'Eugene?' someone shouted from the hall.

Eugene seized his opportunity and bolted from the room, leaving Sidney to get to his feet still holding the poker.

'What's going on, Eugene?' said a male voice.

It was Bertie from number five. He stepped into the room, looking Sidney up and down.

'I saw you barging into young Eugene's,' he said sternly. 'Doesn't seem like a polite way to be acting.'

Sidney shrugged indifference. Bertie stared at the poker in Sidney's hand. Eugene cowered behind the elderly man and then the third male of Finn Close appeared. It was Curtis, and Sidney realised he was outnumbered.

'My daughter has disappeared,' he said.

'And you think the good people of Finn Close have something to do with that?' said Bertie. 'That's a big accusation to be making, Mr Valentine. I'm sorry to hear about your lass, but why don't you allow the police to do their job instead of you barging in here threatening this young lad. I suggest you leave and don't come back, or I will call the police, and you can explain yourself to them.'

Eugene, evidently feeling braver, had eased into his lounge along with Curtis. The three men suddenly looked rather formidable. Sidney gripped the poker, but things could get very messy if he were to use it. He now realised that he'd chosen the wrong house to begin his enquiries. He should have gone to see Eleanor Martinez.

'Fair enough,' he said. 'Sorry to have disturbed you. Believe me, I'll get to the truth.' He set the poker on the fireplace and edged past the line of three. 'I would get yourself some air freshener, Eugene,' he said, 'because there is a terrible stink around here.'

Stepping into the night air, Sidney took a deep breath, looked towards Eleanor's house, and for a moment considered paying her a visit. Glancing behind, he saw Eugene and his guards, arms folded, watching him. Perhaps not, he thought. It was a bit of a hike back to the hotel. He turned up his collar.

'Night, night, gents,' he piped, tapping the side of his nose with his forefinger.

They were still watching him when he reached the lane leading to the main road. A shiver coursed through him, and he thought of Ursula. He'd got no answers from Eugene, but at least he now knew for certain that whatever was going on with the residents of Finn Close, they were in it together.

Chapter 35

The sky was a featureless grey, dawn only minutes old. Ursula's hands were bound behind her with a cable tie. Royston had his thick hand on her arm and led her out of the pod, down three steps and onto a gravel path. She glanced behind her at the wooden building that had been her prison and tried to see beyond it to the neighbouring pod. The screams that had come from within during the night hadn't lasted for long. She guessed that Royston had employed his gaffer tape to quieten whoever had been screaming. Ursula also had been bound and gagged once again when the youth had come to collect her dinner tray.

She tried to ask where she was going, but her voice was muffled beneath the tape around her mouth. Besides, her escort was incapable of putting two words together in reply even if she had managed to ask the question.

Ursula trembled from the cold and from the fear of what might happen. Her legs were unsteady, her feet numb. She'd hardly stood upright for two days. She looked pleadingly at big Royston who seemed to be enjoying himself, despite his two black and swollen eyes. His appearance had her confused. She'd expected one black eye, his left, but she didn't think she had inflicted injury to both.

Was this the point when her time was up? The image of Teddy McNaughten's corpse, a big dagger in his chest, filled her head. Was she about to die? Or was she on her way to the sea where Natalie had met her end? She thought of her father. He'd be lost without her. Who was going to make his tea and supply him with Danish pastries? The man couldn't cope with the modern world to save his life. And what would become of their business? Sidney would never manage it on his own. Dozing in the van every day wouldn't get the job done. And he was useless with technology.

She stumbled where the gravel path met the concrete yard. The farmer with no name waited by his SUV, the passenger door already opened for her. Ursula drew back, whimpering. Royston gripped her arm tightly and ushered her towards the vehicle.

'Morning, missy. A fine day, so it is,' said the farmer with a smile.

Ursula didn't think much of this chauffeur service. Royston, still squeezing her upper arm, forced her to sit in the car. The farmer swung the door closed then climbed behind the wheel. Tears streamed down Ursula's face. She tried to think of escape, but her hands were bound. She couldn't even reach the door handle.

The farmer said nothing further as he manoeuvred his SUV from the yard and onto the lane. They roared up the hill and soon met the junction with the main road. Ursula decided to take a mental note of where they were going. It might make a difference if she got the chance to run, and it forced her to think of ways to escape. Would she offer herself to Royston? Would that be enough? A plaything for the big oaf. Money? She didn't have much but there were those Premium Bonds that Sidney paid into every month. Scream like a banshee until somebody came to her rescue? Not with tape still fixed around her mouth.

They turned left onto Causeway Road and as Ursula pondered their destination, they had soon joined Whitepark Road. All the while, they were getting further from Bushmills, the Armada Hotel and Sidney. Ursula squirmed in her seat, but the farmer seemed quite unruffled. A short time later, he swung the SUV onto a narrower winding road that headed towards the sea. Ursula glimpsed a sign for Ballintoy Harbour, and she cried behind her gag.

At that hour, the small parking area by the harbour was deserted. There wasn't even a boat moored. The SUV slid to a halt by a toilet block. The farmer climbed out and opened the passenger door for Ursula to do the same. She refused to move.

'None of your nonsense, missy,' he said.

How could anyone be so callous, she thought. He was about to kill her yet had the nerve to address her as if they were going for a picnic. He reached in and pulled her arm. It hurt, and she had no option but to tumble out of the car.

She heard another vehicle coming down the hill and her heart leapt in hope of rescue. Now this maniac would get what he deserved. The farmer stepped behind her, and she felt her hands go loose as he cut her binds. Then he removed the gaffer tape from her mouth. Her first instinct was to scream the place down, but the other vehicle rolled into view. It was Royston, and he was driving her white van.

'Right, missy,' said the farmer. 'We'll bid you goodbye.' He had the nerve to smile.

'Please! Don't kill me!'

The farmer chuckled. 'Boyso! We're not into killing anybody, missy. There's your wee van. You can be on your way just as soon as we're gone. I'd be obliged if you kept your wee stay with us to yourself.'

Ursula could hardly believe his cheek, but neither could she manage to reply.

The man climbed back into his SUV and started the engine. Ursula was rooted to the spot. Confusion and relief bubbled in her mind. She watched Royston get out of her van and walk towards her smiling. Well, it was more like a deranged grin; his left eye was closed, the right wasn't much better, but she took it in the spirit it was offered. Holding the van key, he reached out his hand. As she went to take it, he suddenly raised his arm and threw the key towards the rocks by the harbour.

'Ach, Royston, what'd you do that for? That's not nice,' she said as he hurried to the SUV.

He responded to her chiding with a sheepish grin.

'What about my phone?' she called.

The farmer had lowered his window. 'No chance, missy.'

They spun around and roared off as she dashed to retrieve her key.

Chapter 36

Sidney slept later than he'd intended, a consequence of nervous exhaustion but also his long walk of the previous evening. He was awoken at nine by his phone ringing. Constable Dawson had called to tell him that Ursula's disappearance was now officially actioned on the police system and officers would be on the lookout. Sidney thanked him and told him there had been no word from his daughter. He eased from the bed and padded to the bathroom. He lingered under a tepid shower until he could stand no more, towelled himself dry and brushed his teeth. Shaving could wait until he was in the mood. He dressed and tried to formulate a plan for the day ahead, but he was all out of ideas.

Ursula, his only child, whom he'd raised from the age of two, was his pride and joy. He'd only known her mother through a brief fling. A while after that, she had turned up on his doorstep from England one day and presented Ursula to him, claiming she had another life on the stage to pursue. Neither Sidney nor Ursula had clapped eyes on her in years. Sidney had not disputed that he was Ursula's father, although he never had it confirmed by a DNA test. He had raised a pretty daughter to have confidence that helped her to stand up for herself and take care of Sidney too. What would he do without her?

As he sat down to pull on his shoes, there was a knock at the door. He imagined it was housekeeping checking if his room was free for cleaning. With just his left shoe on, he hobbled to the door and pulled it open.

'Well, it's nice to see you're up early and searching for your missing daughter.'

Sidney couldn't summon words, not appropriate ones. 'What the!'

Ursula rushed into his arms and began to cry. 'I thought I would never see you again,' she sobbed.

'Counting your blessings, were you?'

She slapped his arm.

'Don't,' she said. 'I don't think I could take any of your cheek right now.'

'What happened to you?' Sidney asked, leading her inside and closing the door.

'I took a wrong turn,' she said, pulling a tissue from a box on the dressing table and blowing her nose.

Sidney felt his heart pounding. He didn't think he had ever experienced such elation and relief in a single dose.

'I haven't time to explain it all now,' she said. 'We need to call the peelers. I know what's been happening, and I know where Fiona is. But breakfast first, I'm starving.'

She bounded to the door as Sidney followed. They were in the hall heading for the stairs when she stopped and turned.

'Do you not think you should wear both shoes this morning?' She giggled.

Sidney looked at his feet. He turned back to his room, smiling as he went. It was so good to hear his daughter's laughter.

They tucked into a cooked breakfast in the hotel dining room, while Ursula regaled Sidney of her experience at the hands of a nameless farmer and his wonky son. As she did so, Sidney called Martin Dawson to tell him that Ursula had turned up safe and well. Sidney then suggested that they meet urgently. Since they were now in possession of information that could be vital to a police murder inquiry, he also requested the presence of DI Kelso.

As the chat continued over their breakfast, Sidney, already on his third coffee of the morning, told Ursula of his efforts to find her.

'Were you really worried about me, Daddy?'

'Of course, I was frantic with worry.'

'Ach, it's nice to know that you care about me,' she said.

Sidney told her about his visit to Finn Close the night before.

'Seems as though that entire street is up to no good,' he said.

'It explains why I saw Julie going to that farm. Everything must be connected to the lottery win. I'm certain that someone was being held in the pod next to mine. They screamed the place down. I reckon the sods have kidnapped Fiona to get their hands on the money.'

'Or treasure,' said Sidney.

'Treasure?'

'I haven't told you about my visit to the museum the other day. I spoke to the archaeologist who'd met with Teddy McNaughten about the *Girona*. It seems quite likely that Teddy had got his hands on treasure, or at least knew where to find it, before he was murdered. He'd shown Dr MacIntosh a few items, including weapons. They could be the same weapons that were used to kill Teddy and Natalie.'

Their conversation was interrupted when a flustered-looking DI Kelso marched into the dining room and stood before them, hands on her hips. She didn't appear dressed for work, the gym most likely, but it didn't alter her expression – peeved.

'Mr Valentine, you continue to monopolise police resources in this town. What is it now?'

'Well, for starters, my daughter has turned up, alive and well, no thanks to you.'

'Yes, I can see that,' said Kelso, somehow without acknowledging Ursula's presence.

'Well,' said Sidney, unwilling to permit the cop to sneer any further, 'Ursula has something important to tell you. And you're going to listen to us for a change.'

The cop simpered but pulled a chair over and sat down.

'Go ahead, I can hardly wait.'

Chapter 37

DI Kelso's eyes widened on hearing Ursula's story. It was debatable whether the cop believed a single word, but she did appear to listen.

'Right,' she said when she'd heard enough. 'I think you better show me where all this drama took place.'

When they went outside, Sidney saw Constable Dawson seated at the wheel of a marked police car.

'Get in, we'll take you,' said Kelso.

Sidney and Ursula climbed into the back while the detective sat in the front.

'Good morning, Sidney,' said Dawson. 'I'm glad to see your daughter has turned up.' He smiled warmly at Ursula who felt a rush of blood at being greeted by such a handsome guy.

She managed to smile back.

'Do you know each other?' said Kelso. She glared at the constable.

'We met in the hotel bar, isn't that right, son?' said Sidney.

'My sister works in there, ma'am,' said Dawson.

'Drive on,' Kelso ordered, unimpressed.

Ursula had no problem directing them to the farm lane off Causeway Road. They drove uphill, but as they reached the brow and descended towards the farm, Ursula sensed that something was different though she couldn't think what it was.

When they pulled into the farmyard, she saw the farmer with no name coming out of his kitchen. He stood, hands in his boilersuit pockets watching as the party emerged from the police vehicle. DI Kelso strode towards him, the rest ambling behind.

'Ach, good morning, Mr Robinson,' said Kelso, cheerfully. 'For a minute there I didn't realise this was your place.'

The farmer smiled, his fat cheeks glowing.

'Inspector Kelso, how's things?' said Robinson, gazing at Ursula, Sidney and Constable Dawson but showing no signs that he recognised anyone.

Ursula went straight to overheat.

'How's it going?' she yelped. 'Is that all you have to say? You held me prisoner here!'

'Quiet please,' said Kelso. 'I'll handle this.'

'But–?' Ursula tried.

'I said be quiet!' Kelso turned again to the farmer.

'Sorry to bother you, Mr Robinson, but we've had a complaint. This young woman claims she was abducted and kept here against her will for more than twenty-four hours. Would you care to respond to that?'

Robinson smiled at Ursula, his eyes twinkling.

'Boyso, missy. I think you've got the wrong man here. I think I'd remember meeting such a lovely lass as you.'

'Missy! That's what he called me! He knows rightly.' Ursula couldn't believe what was happening. 'Get Royston out here. He'll remember. He's the one who tied me up.'

'Be quiet, Ursula!' Kelso snapped.

'But you can't just take his word for it. He's lying. He stuck me in one of those damn glamping pods, handcuffed me, gagged me and locked me in. I reckon that Fiona McCabe is being kept here too. She was in the pod next to me.'

Ursula watched as Sidney looked around him, then DI Kelso and Dawson joined in. She glared at the farmer who maintained his smug grin. Then finally she also looked.

'Where are these glamping pods?' Kelso asked her.

Ursula pointed to the open space where three glamping pods in the style of gypsy caravans were curiously absent.

'They were right here, honest,' she said, her eyes staring in hope, her mind in chaos.

The farmer still said nothing.

DI Kelso winced, but to her credit, she kept going.

'Know anything about glamping pods, Mr Robinson?'

'Aye, I do indeed,' he replied. 'We build them here, a wee sideline for us, if you know what I mean. Diversification, the government calls it. The boys from Dunluce Joinery Works do most of the hard graft and we finish them off. We sell them all around the country, you know, but we haven't built any lately.'

Ursula spotted Royston coming out of a barn and strolling towards the farmhouse.

'Hey, Royston! Remember me?'

The youth glanced across the yard, then dropped his head and hurried into the kitchen.

'You see,' said Ursula, now in some desperation. 'He knows who I am. He should do; he certainly enjoyed staring at these.' She indicated her breasts.

'As you know, Inspector Kelso, our Royston doesn't speak,' said Robinson. 'I don't see how he would know the young lass, unless you were the person driving the wee van that made a wrong turn in the lane the other day. I saw it from the barn; Royston was trying to get past in the tractor.'

Ursula cupped a hand over her mouth in horror.

'Can't believe you're doing this,' she said. 'What about Fiona? I bet she's still here,' she tried, looking for understanding from the detective.

Kelso glared in the manner Ursula and Sidney had come to expect. Then she turned to Dawson.

'Take a look around, Constable,' she said. 'That's if you don't mind, Mr Robinson?'

'No bother at all,' the farmer replied. 'Can I offer you some tea while you're waiting?'

'No thanks, we've already taken up enough of your time,' said Kelso.

'I can tell you exactly what that kitchen is like,' said Ursula. 'There's a big table in the middle, and they drink out of blue-and-white mugs and eat chocolate digestives.'

No one was taking much notice of what Ursula was saying now. They watched as Dawson went from one outbuilding to the next, clearly finding nothing suspicious. Ursula wandered to the spot where she knew three gypsy caravans had stood. It was a rectangular gravelled area, but she found nothing to indicate that glamping pods had been there earlier that morning. Then she remembered one more thing that she hadn't mentioned to the detective. She rushed over to join the group.

'Julie! She was here the day I was abducted. I'd followed her. She went into one of the pods. We can ask her; she'll confirm that they were standing right here.'

'Do you know anything about that, Mr Robinson?' Kelso asked, now sounding very embarrassed.

The farmer shook his head as if he were puzzled.

'Can't say I know a Julie,' he replied. 'When was this you say?'

'Two days ago!' Ursula barked.

Robinson shook his head again slowly. 'No. Like I say, we had no pods here two days ago.'

Constable Dawson rejoined them in the farmyard.

'Nothing, ma'am,' he said, shaking his head.

An eerie silence ensued as DI Kelso gazed around her.

'You're certain you haven't met Miss Valentine before?' she asked the farmer.

'No, I'm sorry to say. But she's very welcome here anytime.'

'No chance,' Ursula scoffed.

'Is there anyone else at the farm who Miss Valentine might be confusing with you?'

'There's only me and Royston just now. The wife's visiting her mother in Tyrone.'

DI Kelso winced.

'OK, thanks for your time, Mr Robinson.'

'No bother, Inspector.'

Ursula could have sworn the farmer winked at her, but it was pointless to stand there and argue. It was his word against hers. He'd been a shrewd man, getting those pods off his farm before she'd returned with the cops.

'Thanks for your time, Mr Robinson,' Ursula said in a mocking voice.

'Back in the car, you two,' Kelso ordered.

Sidney, who'd been silent throughout the exchange, guided his daughter to the police car before she got herself into more trouble. Not a word was said on the drive back to Bushmills, except as they drove past the lane leading to Finn Close.

'Are we not going to speak to Julie now?' Ursula asked. 'She'll confirm that the glamping pods were on the farm two days ago.'

Kelso didn't reply to Ursula's question and instructed Dawson to drive on by. Ursula fumed. When they pulled up outside the Armada Hotel, the detective turned to face father and daughter.

'I really don't know what's been going on with you two,' she said. 'You have just wasted my Saturday morning with hare-brained stories of kidnapping. I'm trying to find the murderer of two people and your shenanigans are obstructing my investigation. So, here's what you're going to do. You go into that hotel, pack up your stuff and go home, right now. If I see you in this area again, I will arrest you for obstructing a police inquiry. Is that understood?'

'I can't believe you just took that man's word over mine,' said Ursula.

Sidney nudged her to be quiet.

'Is that understood?' Kelso repeated.

Sidney and Ursula were silent.

'Right,' said Kelso, 'get out. I'll be checking later that you've gone.'

Sidney held back as Ursula got out of the car.

'One thing puzzles me, Inspector Kelso,' he said.

'Only one? I am surprised,' said the cop.

'Did you like Teddy McNaughten?'

Her face flushed. 'What on earth do you mean?'

'I gather that you grew up in the same street.'

'How do you know that?'

'I'm a detective,' said Sidney. 'But I was thinking that if you perhaps hated Teddy McNaughten from your childhood days, you might not be trying so hard to find his killer. Or indeed, if you hated him so much, you might have had a motive for killing him yourself.' Sidney saw Kelso flinch in her seat. 'Two murders and a missing person and it seems you still have nothing.'

Sidney didn't believe it possible for a face to produce such an ice-cold stare, but Kelso's had no difficulty.

'I will catch the killer, Mr Valentine. You can be sure of that. As for your missing person, if I were you, I would consult your client. All this time and she still has not officially reported her sister as missing. Why is that? She has you two running around up here like a pair of delinquent glue-sniffers, accusing innocent people of all sorts. Go home to Belfast and think very carefully about ever coming back here.'

'It's Holywood.'

'Whatever. Goodbye, Mr Valentine.'

* * *

Ursula had waited by the hotel entrance for Sidney to finish his conversation.

'What was all that about?' she asked.

'Nothing important.'

They watched as the police car drove away.

'I suppose we better go and pack,' said Ursula.

'We can pack, but we're not going home,' said Sidney. 'I fancy a wee change of scenery. Somewhere out of this town but not too far away.'

Chapter 38

Even Ursula was surprised at Sidney's renewed determination to find the truth of what had been going on around the Giant's Causeway.

'The north coast,' he said as they departed the Armada Hotel, 'is supposed to be a place for holidays and day trips. How is anyone supposed to relax when there's been two murders and a disappearance, and no one wants to speak the truth? They're not getting away with it.'

'Yes, Daddy,' was all Ursula could say in response. She'd already booked them into an exclusive country hotel a mile outside Ballycastle. Hopefully, this location was far enough from Finn Close and Bushmills to keep them out of reach of a tetchy DI Kelso.

'I can't believe that detective,' said Ursula. 'Why didn't she question Julie?'

'Don't worry about that.'

Ursula nearly collided with a hedge when she turned to glare at her father.

'You're sounding very chilled about all this,' she said.

Travelling inland via the Straid Road, Ballycastle was twelve miles east of Bushmills. Not far out of town, they entered a sweeping lane and were instantly treated to a view of a magnificent oasis standing on high ground in open countryside. The Atlantic Ocean, calm and blue, captured their attention. They gazed towards Rathlin Island, a few miles off the coast, and the afternoon ferry venturing out from Ballycastle harbour. On such a clear day, they could see north-east all the way to the Mull of Kintyre. Their latest accommodation tended towards luxury, costing more than Sidney would ever consider paying for a hotel stay, but he'd decided that after her recent incarceration, Ursula might appreciate a little pampering. She had been incredulous when she found it online and he had agreed to the price. Now she could enjoy a sumptuous room, excellent food and a relaxing spa. There was, of course, still work to be done.

Ursula's bewilderment at Sidney's laid-back attitude continued all through the checking-in process, and by the time the two of them settled down to an early dinner in the swanky restaurant, she was bursting to know what he was thinking.

'Daddy, would you mind telling me why we're doing all this? I thought after what happened to me, we'd be high-tailing it home.'

Sidney continued to browse the menu; aware he was slowly winding his daughter up. He waited until a waitress had taken their order then sipped his wine and grinned.

'Daddy! For goodness' sake.'

'OK,' he began, 'to quote the famous Mr Rumsfeld, "As we know, there are known knowns; there are things we know we know. We also know there are known unknowns; that is to say we know there are some things we do not know. But there are also unknown unknowns – the ones we don't know we don't know. And… it is the latter category that tends to be the difficult ones." But I can't believe you haven't picked up on this.'

She fired him a sulky stare.

'Firstly, that farm where you were held prisoner. Wasn't the farmer's name Robinson?'

'So?'

'Didn't that couple, Cissy and Bertie, say they were retired farmers? Their son had taken over the running of their farm, and isn't their name Robinson?'

'OMG! I didn't realise.'

'It's OK, you can thank me later.'

Ursula digested the information for a moment.

'That means,' she said, 'Cissy and Bertie have known Fiona's whereabouts all this time, assuming that she is the person I heard screaming in the pod alongside the one I was in. Julie left Curtis off at a joinery works in Bushmills, and then I followed her to the farm. Had she been bringing food to Fiona? And, according to that nasty farmer, Curtis works for the company that builds those flipping pods. They're all in it together.'

'That's what I told you. All we have to do now is gather some proof without getting caught by DI Kelso.'

'What about rescuing Fiona?' said Ursula. 'The pods are gone, but they must be keeping her somewhere on the farm. We can't just leave her there.'

This was the stage when Sidney's face seemed to cloud over.

'I think we need to speak to her sister again,' he said. 'Eve hasn't been honest with us. She still has questions to answer.'

'What else?'

'What do you mean?' said Sidney.

'You said firstly and went on to talk about the Robinsons. So, you must have a secondly and maybe a thirdly in your list.'

'All right, I get the idea, Ursula.'

She waited, amused, as her father struggled to get his thoughts in order.

'Oh yes,' he said at last. 'Secondly, as I just said, we need a word with Eve. And thirdly, I want to speak to Eleanor the history teacher.'

'What for?'

'As well as DI Kelso, Eleanor grew up in the same street as Teddy McNaughten. It might be useful to get her take on things. And, in case you're going to ask, there isn't a fourthly.'

Ursula cleared her throat, and a bemused grin emerged on her face.

'What?' said Sidney.

'Prepare to be shocked,' she whispered. 'Don't look now, but our client has just come in for dinner.'

Sidney did the opposite; he turned and gazed at the figure of Eve McCabe as a waitress showed her to a table.

'What was I just saying about unknown unknowns?' he said.

Chapter 39

'You have some explaining to do, Eve love,' said Ursula, stealing a chip from the woman's plate.

Father and daughter slid into the booth either side of the woman. She gazed from one to the other through her enormous specs and managed to hold a startled expression. But innocence wasn't going to cut it for the private detectives.

'Any time you're ready,' Sidney said. 'And it better be good, because I'm very close to telling you to take your business elsewhere.'

'I don't know who you are or what you want with me, but if you don't leave me alone, I'll call for the manager.' She attempted to continue with her meal, but Sidney placed his hand on hers.

'Waitress!' Eve called.

A young woman approached the table.

'Can you get the manager, please?'

'Is there a problem, Miss McCabe?' the waitress asked.

'Yes, these people are disturbing me.'

Sidney and Ursula smiled at the waitress who looked in a quandary over what to do next.

'Please hurry,' continued Eve. 'I'll scream the place down if you don't get these people away from me.'

The waitress bolted from the restaurant.

'You're certainly a woman who's full of surprises,' said Sidney as he rose from the table. 'I'll send you the final bill for our expenses. Come on, Ursula, let's finish our dinner.'

'I have no idea what you're talking about. Please just leave me alone.'

Sidney was still shaking his head in disbelief when they returned to their own table. He and Ursula seemed to have lost their appetite for dessert.

'I have never in my life met a woman like her. She's completely off her trolley,' said Sidney. 'Imagine paying us two and a half grand up front to find her sister then when we try to provide updates and get more information from her, she denies even knowing us.'

Ursula saw a man in a dark suit stride into the restaurant and go directly to Eve's table. She watched as Eve nodded towards them, and the man turned to look. A few seconds later, he was standing by their table.

'Good evening, sir and miss, I'm the restaurant duty manager,' he said with a polite smile and lightweight voice. He looked little more than twenty, with a slight build, acne, and a shirt too big at the collar. 'Is there a problem? Only the lady across there has complained that you were harassing her.'

'Sorry, bit of a misunderstanding, that's all. We won't be bothering the lady again,' said Sidney.

'We do have a zero tolerance regarding guests who upset other guests during their stay with us.'

'Understood,' said Sidney.

The man smiled, almost bowed, then strolled off, casting his gaze around the restaurant as if on the lookout for further violations of hotel policy.

While Sidney finished his wine, Ursula kept an eye on the peculiar woman who had hired them. She ate alone, without even looking around her or browsing a phone as lone diners were often prone to do. Sidney already seemed to have washed his hands completely of the woman and her plight, but Ursula, realising this was not the place for confrontation, intended to challenge her as soon as she had an opportunity, perhaps away from the hotel. They may no longer have a paid interest in this case, but they still wanted answers. It was her who had been abducted and held prisoner in a glamping pod. She might well have been killed, and for what? No way was Eve simply going to carry on without explanation.

* * *

Next morning, Ursula had a swim and a spell in the jacuzzi, intending to join Sidney, a habitual late riser, afterwards for breakfast. Relaxing in the warmth of the gurgling pool, she watched amused as Eve padded in, wearing a hotel bathrobe and slippers. The woman seemed unaware of Ursula's presence. She slipped off her robe, revealing a slim figure in a black one-piece swimsuit, and stepped into the swimming pool still wearing her big glasses. Immediately, using breaststroke, she began swimming lengths of the short pool. Ursula was tempted to join her but didn't wish to provoke any tantrums from the puzzling woman. Instead, she got on with her relaxing and, as she'd hoped, a few minutes later, the woman stepped into the jacuzzi seemingly without recognising her company.

'Morning,' Ursula chimed above the rumble of the water. The woman, who'd sat with her eyes closed, now peered at Ursula.

'Not you,' she said. 'Just leave me alone, please.'

Ursula chuckled. 'I was in here first, love.'

'Well, please don't talk to me. I don't know who you are, and I have nothing to say to you.'

'But I know who you are, Fiona.'

Chapter 40

Sidney was reading a Sunday paper in a bright lounge that overlooked the green fields that stretched to the ocean. Ursula bounced in, looking chuffed with herself. Sidney glanced at her then did a retake when he noticed the woman standing beside his daughter.

'Morning, Daddy, look who I found.'

'What's going on?' Sidney asked, gazing from one woman to the other.

Ursula invited her companion to sit as Sidney continued to look confused.

'Had a change of mind?' he said drily.

Ursula giggled.

'Daddy, we made a bit of a mistake last night. Meet Fiona, long-lost sister of Eve.'

'Fiona?'

The woman who Ursula had identified as Fiona smiled sheepishly. Her brown hair was still wet, and evidently she wore the same style of large-framed glasses as her sister.

'Hello,' said Fiona.

'Yes, Daddy,' said Ursula with a grin. 'Twins. You can close your mouth now.'

Despite her agreeing to meet them and to resolve the issue of mistaken identity, Fiona seemed reluctant to engage any further.

'We've been looking for you,' said Sidney. 'Your sister hired us to find you.'

'Now that you've found me,' Fiona said, 'will you please leave me alone. I don't want anyone to know where I am.'

'But we have to tell Eve,' Sidney said. 'She's been worried about you.'

'Has she?'

'Yes, of course.'

Fiona dropped her gaze and began to fidget with a silver ring on her right middle finger.

'Please don't tell her where I am. Just tell her that you've found me, nothing more.'

'What's been going on, Fiona?' Ursula asked. 'Were you kidnapped and held on the Robinson farm?'

The woman's eyes widened, looking very frightened behind the huge lenses. Ursula didn't wait for an answer.

'You were being held in a glamping pod next to me, weren't you?' she said. 'I heard you screaming the place down. How did you get away? Why were those people keeping you prisoner?'

Fiona jumped to her feet, trembling and looking very upset. 'I don't have to tell you anything. I don't know who you are or what you want with me. And I certainly don't want you telling my sister where I am.'

She hurried from the lounge. Fortunately for Sidney and Ursula, there was no hotel staff around to witness the confrontation.

Sidney was shaking his head in despair again.

'That went well,' said Ursula.

'Let's have breakfast and then get out of here,' said Sidney. 'Our work is done. We found Fiona.'

Ursula cleared her throat, smiled and cocked her head to the side. 'Excuse me, but I was the one who found Fiona.'

'I was thinking the same as you,' said Sidney.

'No, you weren't. I saw the look on your face when I brought Fiona in just now. You hadn't a baldy notion what was going on.'

During breakfast, they speculated on the relationship between the identical sisters. They also kept an eye out for another appearance by Fiona in the dining room.

'On the way home this morning,' said Sidney, 'we'll stop at the Garden of Eden and tell Eve that we found her twin sister, another little detail that she had failed to share with us.'

'Are you planning on telling her where to find Fiona?'

'I haven't decided. I'm not sure what good it will do. Besides, Fiona doesn't know or trust us. She's likely to leave here now and find somewhere else to hide.'

'But what has she been hiding from?' said Ursula. 'She wasn't happy at us finding her and that we have been working for Eve. She wouldn't even admit to being held prisoner on that farm.'

'Makes you wonder who is in the right in all of this,' said Sidney.

'But what does Fiona have to fear from her sister?'

'About time we asked Eve a few probing questions.'

'That's if we can find her,' said Ursula.

Sidney smirked.

'You don't think that Eve and Fiona are one and the same?' he said.

'Ach, Daddy.'

Chapter 41

They checked out of the hotel directly after breakfast. Before leaving, they wandered through the resident's areas in the hope of meeting Fiona again. Maybe she had calmed down and would be more willing to discuss her situation. But there was no sign of her, and the hotel receptionist politely refused to give them Fiona's room number.

'It's not the cheapest of places to hide yourself away,' Sidney mused, examining his bill for their overnight stay. 'I hope Eve is prepared to cover our expenses.'

'She hired us,' said Ursula. 'She told us she was prepared to pay whatever it took to find Fiona. And we found her.'

'But will it be sufficient for us to tell her that? I imagine that she's expecting to see Fiona, or at least to be told where she is.'

'Which brings us back to the question, who do we trust?'

Ursula drove them south towards Belfast. Early morning showers had developed to a constant drizzle by the time she stopped the van outside Eve's bungalow in Eden. Sidney, refreshed from his snooze on the journey, quickly got out and bounded to the front door of the house. It appeared his temper had simmered all morning, even when asleep. He was about to demand truthful answers to his questions. Ursula knew that an irritated Sidney was a beast to be feared and admired, although she usually just admired.

When Eve opened her door, Sidney barged inside without greeting.

'Hello, Eve,' Ursula said to compensate for her father's brashness.

'Do you have news for me?' Eve asked indicating the door to the lounge.

Sidney didn't require the invitation. He'd already flopped into an armchair. Ursula knew he would soon request a cup of tea.

Eve remained on her feet, nervously caressing her hands as Ursula swept her eyes around a room cluttered with newspapers, books and a myriad of porcelain ornaments upon the fireplace, windowsill and sideboard. It was a lounge reminiscent of the seventies, or perhaps even the sixties. The only nod to modern times was the huge TV screen and Sky Q box beneath.

'Some questions first,' Sidney snapped. 'And I want the truth, Eve, or we're out of here and our business arrangement is over.'

The woman attempted a smile, but it somehow floundered.

'And tea would be good,' he said.

Eve flinched but said nothing and went straight to her kitchen. Ursula followed, ordering Sidney to stay put. She watched as Eve filled a kettle and switched it on to boil and placed tea bags into three mugs.

'You know, Eve,' Ursula said, 'what I can't understand is why you even bothered to hire us and then failed to share vital information.'

'No, I didn't.'

'Yes, you did. Why didn't you mention that Fiona is your twin?'

'I suppose I should have told you that, but we don't even look like sisters.'

'Fiona looks exactly like you,' Ursula exclaimed. 'You even wear the same type of glasses.'

Eve shrugged.

'Sorry,' she said.

'Why would Fiona not want you to know where she is?' Ursula asked.

'You've found her? You know where she is? You have to tell me.'

'No, I don't. Your sister is afraid of something or someone and that seems to include you. If you won't tell me what's been going on, then I'm not revealing her whereabouts.'

Eve stamped her foot like a petulant teenager. 'But I paid you to find her. You have to tell me.'

Ursula shook her head.

'It doesn't work like that. We don't know what's been going on. If you keep information from us, then we can't trust you. Worse still, we could be putting more lives at risk, including our own. I have already been abducted by a crazy farmer and his son.'

Tears spewed from the woman as she abandoned her task. To Ursula, she was behaving like she'd always gotten her own way and resorted to tears and tantrums when she didn't.

'It's just typical of Fiona!' Eve cried. 'It's always been about her. She was Mum's favourite in every little thing. New trainers? Fiona was first. Boyzone tickets? Fiona and her friends, not me. It's just not fair. She always gets what she wants. And now she has you on her side.'

'We're not taking sides, Eve,' Ursula said patiently. 'Two people are dead. I was abducted, and I believe Fiona was too. She is obviously afraid of something. You must tell us what this is really all about.'

'OK, I'm sorry.' Eve sniffed back tears and resumed making the tea.

A silence ensued while the woman gradually composed herself. She and Ursula carried mugs of tea and a plate of biscuits into the lounge.

'Well?' Sidney asked.

'I think Eve realises that we can't help her if she isn't honest with us,' said Ursula.

She looked for validation from the teary-eyed woman. Eve sat on the edge of her sofa cradling a mug of tea in her hands.

'Isn't that right, Eve?' Ursula prompted.

'I suppose so.'

'Why don't you start at the beginning,' said Sidney.

Ursula shook her head as if to suggest that would not be such a good idea. Eve harboured grievances from childhood and was likely to begin with sisterly brawls in their mother's womb. It was clear now to Ursula that the twins were not close, loving siblings.

'Maybe just start with the real reason why you hired us,' Ursula suggested.

Eve sniffed. 'Fiona won the lottery.'

Chapter 42

'She's keeping all the money,' Eve sobbed, grappling for a box of tissues on her coffee table.

Sidney grimaced at Ursula. The revelation hardly came as a surprise, since on their first day in Finn Close, Cissy had told Ursula that Fiona had taken all the money.

'But you told us that you knew nothing about the lottery syndicate,' Sidney said.

'I know, and I'm sorry. I thought that if I told you it was all about an argument over winning the lottery, you wouldn't have agreed to help me.'

'Tell us what happened,' said Ursula, trying to remain sympathetic while thinking of two murders and her abduction.

'Fiona told me a year ago that she was running a lottery syndicate with her friends and neighbours. I asked if I could join.' Eve reached for another tissue. 'At first, she said no. Can you believe it? Her twin sister. I felt hurt, but it was no big deal, and no surprise either. Fiona has been like that our whole lives. Selfish. It's always been about her, and not us. It surprises me that she would even do the lottery in a syndicate, but she did. Then one day she called me and said that if I still wanted to join, I could. She told me that some guy in her street didn't always pay his share, and I could take his place.'

'Would that be Eugene, the postman?' Ursula asked.

'I think so. He hardly ever paid his entry money but still expected to hear if they had won anything. A few weeks ago, when there had been a rollover draw, I phoned Fiona to ask how we'd done. She told me she hadn't checked and would let me know. You see, Fiona usually chose the numbers although she'd told everyone that she just played the lucky dip. Of course, it meant that each week none of us were told the syndicate's numbers. Knowing Fiona well, I suspected that she wasn't telling me everything. I guessed that apart from playing the lucky dip for the syndicate, she also played some lines for herself.'

'But if you didn't know the numbers, what convinced you that you'd won?' Sidney asked.

'Eventually, Fiona told me that she'd won; not the syndicate, only her. She'd won twenty-three million pounds, and she was intending to keep it all. I didn't believe her, and I told her so. I could always tell when she was lying. Her tone becomes frivolous. When we were kids, no matter what she lied about, she always deflected it to me. If Mum had been getting at her for not doing her homework, she turned the attention to me and told Mum I'd been smoking, or I'd been with a boy in his bedroom. None of that was ever true. If Fiona didn't come home after being out clubbing, she would insist to Mum that she'd told me to pass on the message when she hadn't. She has always been a liar and a cheat. As soon as she claimed it was her winning line and not the syndicate's, I knew she was lying. And, of course, she deflected it to me by saying I had an evil and suspicious mind.'

'It would be difficult to prove she was lying,' said Ursula. 'What did you do?'

'Fiona told me that her neighbours were threatening her and demanding a share of the winnings. I had no sympathy and told her she would get what she deserved. Then, a day or so later, I couldn't get hold of her. I thought she'd already taken the money and run. That's when I hired you to find her. I had also contacted some of the others in the syndicate. I didn't really know them well except that they were either Fiona's neighbours or people she worked with.'

'Which members did you contact?' Sidney asked.

'It was easy to get hold of a phone number for Fiona's boss Teddy. I told him that I believed Fiona was lying and she was intending to keep all the money. He sounded relaxed about it, but said he would have a word with her. Then Fiona disappeared, and I heard nothing from Teddy. Next thing was you told me he'd been killed.'

'Do you think Fiona had something to do with his murder?' Sidney asked.

Eve burst into tears once again, and Ursula quickly supplied the tissues.

'What am I supposed to think?' Eve sobbed. 'I reckon my beloved sister would do anything to keep that money for herself.'

'Who else did you speak to in the syndicate?' Sidney asked.

'I found a number on my phone for one of Fiona's neighbours. I sent her a text telling her what Fiona was up to. She replied, saying she didn't believe that Fiona would do that to her friends. She promised to speak to her.'

'And who was this?' Ursula asked.

'Her name was Natalie. Isn't that the woman whose body was found on the Giant's Causeway?'

Sidney and Ursula looked at each other. The two people Eve had spoken to about her sister's intentions to cheat the syndicate out of a fortune were now dead.

'Now, are you going to tell me where my sister is hiding?' said Eve.

Chapter 43

Sidney made no secret of his delight at being home. He sank into his recliner and savoured the view across Belfast Lough as the Cairnryan ferry eased by. Ursula poured her father a double whiskey and an IPA for herself and joined him by the window. It only took a few minutes before her curiosity overcame her, and she called a number on her brand-new mobile. Sidney, close to nodding off, still managed to listen as Ursula made her enquiry.

'Thanks for your help,' she said, ending the call.

'Well?'

'Just as we expected. The hotel receptionist said that Miss McCabe checked out this morning. We've lost her again.'

'If what Eve told us is true then Fiona is a very rich woman. She can go wherever she likes.'

'And if she's a double murderer?' said Ursula.

'You don't believe that, do you?'

'I'm not sure. If Teddy or Natalie had tried to stop Fiona running away with a fortune, then she had motive to kill them. But why would she hang around on the north coast if she had loads of dosh and she'd just murdered two people? And why, if she was not prepared to share the money with the other syndicate members, did she not simply leave straight away? It doesn't make sense. Besides that, I still reckon Fiona was being held prisoner in the glamping pod next to mine. Surely, if those rogues suspected her of murder, they would have handed her over to the police. Instead, they kept her as a prisoner and it seems were trying to extort money from her, albeit money they believed was rightfully theirs.'

Sidney took a welcome sip from his glass. He turned towards Ursula and with an impish smile said, 'You do realise what you are saying, daughter?'

'What?'

'There are still two murders to be solved.'

'But they have nothing to do with us, Daddy. Eve has paid us for our work, although we can't now tell her where her sister has gone. Isn't it time we got back to counting potholes?'

'I'm surprised at you, Ursula Valentine.'

He sat back, sipped his whiskey and gazed through the window. Ursula chuckled to herself but didn't reply. She knew her father wouldn't leave things as they now stood. Two unsolved murders and a woman who'd gone AWOL again was simply too much for Sidney to ignore.

* * *

It came as no surprise to Ursula the next morning that once he'd had his breakfast, Sidney suggested they get on the road north once again.

'I didn't think the Giant's Causeway was within our area for a pothole survey,' she teased.

'Ha ha, very droll.'

'Where exactly are we going?'

'Firstly, I want a chat with that history teacher Eleanor Martinez. She is the only person living in Finn Close who doesn't seem to bother with the rest. But she also grew up in the same street as Teddy McNaughten. It would be interesting to hear her views on all that has happened recently.'

'And secondly?'

'What?'

'You said firstly, so there must be a secondly.'

'Don't start that again, Ursula.'

'Well?'

'OK, so we begin another search for Fiona. She remains at the centre of all this nonsense and, considering what Eve eventually shared with us, I have some questions I'd now like Fiona to answer.'

'How do we start searching again? We can't storm into Finn Close asking questions, not when we know what those people are capable of.'

'Fiona, for some reason, has been hiding locally. Why? She must have good reason. So, if she's checked out of one hotel in the area, she has probably moved to another.'

'Are we going to search every hotel on the north coast? That could take ages.'

'We can telephone most of them. Just ask to speak with a guest named Fiona McCabe. If she's not staying there, we apologise for the mistake. If she is, then we hang up and go and see her face to face before she scarpers again.'

'Ach, Daddy, you've been thinking hard about this.'

'I'm not as stupid as you look, my dear.'

She gave his arm a slap.

'Let's hope Fiona doesn't resort to a fake name, though, or your plan won't work. And we'll have to be careful,' she warned. 'I don't fancy crossing that DI Kelso again. She's not a very nice policewoman.'

Chapter 44

Sidney and Ursula were slouching in their van, parked close to the gates of the high school in Coleraine where Eleanor Martinez was a history teacher. They thought it best to meet the woman as she left school rather than visit her at Finn Close. Sidney hoped that Eleanor would prove more talkative in a neutral environment. It also allowed them to avoid the prying eyes of other Finn Close residents. Ursula had begun the task of phoning local hotels to check if Fiona McCabe was a guest. Once they discovered where Fiona was staying, Ursula proposed that they check into the same hotel. Ursula pictured the look on the woman's face when they met again. Several attempts so far, however, had yielded nothing. Ursula's low boredom threshold had been breached after the third call.

It was a cold afternoon; wet and windy. Parents who'd arrived to collect their children after school were unlikely to linger for a chat. Sidney watched carefully for Eleanor

Martinez to emerge from the school building. Ursula wasn't entirely confident of his strategy.

'This is an awfully big school, and there's more than one entrance. We could easily miss Eleanor leaving.'

'That's why when the bell goes, you're going to cover one gate, and I'll take another.'

'We can see the school car park from here. Why don't we just wait by her car?'

'Good idea.' Sidney climbed out of the van. 'Come on before we miss the woman,' he said, closing the door.

Ursula caught up with him in the driveway leading to the school's main entrance and the car park located on the right. The bell for the end of the day had just sounded, and kids suddenly poured from every exit and swarmed towards them. Soon they were engulfed by students. There seemed little chance of them spotting one teacher as she left the building, and they hadn't yet located Eleanor's car. They were nearing the entrance to the main building when Ursula stopped dead.

'Oh no!'

'What is it?' Sidney asked.

'Too late, I think.'

Sidney gazed to the spot that held Ursula's attention. DI Kelso was looking right at them.

'What the heck is she doing here?' Sidney muttered. 'That woman gets everywhere.'

They were only twenty yards away, but the police detective was already scowling.

'I would guess she is collecting her daughter from school,' said Ursula, trying her best to smile at the cop. 'I hope you have a plausible explanation ready or we're in big trouble.'

'Keep going, pretend you haven't noticed her.'

'Great idea. Is that all you have, Daddy?'

Kelso's hands had gone to her hips in her habitual cop stance. Clearly, it wasn't confined to her duty hours. It was too late for them to simply ignore the woman.

'Is she not a bit old for school, Mr Valentine?' Kelso said with a smirk. She also did her best not to look at Ursula.

'Didn't picture you as the maternal type, Inspector Kelso,' said Sidney with a grin. He nodded to the young girl standing next to the cop.

The twelve-year-old looked remarkably like her mother. She had a similar hairstyle and the same scowl on her face.

It was a woman approaching them who was next to speak.

'Mr Valentine, have you come to see me?' said Eleanor Martinez.

'Wait a minute,' said Kelso. 'You two know each other? Yes, of course you do. I should have realised. Are you all right with this, Eleanor?'

'Wait a minute,' said Sidney. 'You two know each other? Yes, of course you do. Raised in the same street, isn't that right?'

Kelso glared at father and daughter, then winced. 'I know that you're aware I can't simply arrest the pair of you right now but, I swear, just give me one good reason and I'll have you on prison food within the hour. I'll see you, Eleanor. Let's go, Lisa,' she said, ushering her daughter away.

'How can I help you, Mr Valentine?' Eleanor asked.

Sidney introduced Ursula to the history teacher who smiled warmly and shook Ursula's hand.

'Since we are now aware of what has been going on in Finn Close,' Sidney explained, 'we were wondering if we could get your insight on the matter.'

The woman suddenly turned pale. She clutched at a gold pendant she was wearing on a chain around her neck.

'I see,' she said hesitantly. 'And what do you want to know?'

'Are you aware of the conspiracy to extort lottery winnings from Fiona McCabe?'

Eleanor smiled at last.

'I told you they were up to no good,' she said.

'What we can't figure out is why Teddy McNaughten and Natalie MacDonnell would have been murdered over it.'

'But it's all down to Fiona McCabe, don't you see?' said Eleanor. 'She's to blame for all the trouble. She won't stop until she gets everything.'

Sidney couldn't help looking perplexed.

'I don't understand, Eleanor,' he said.

'But you just said you know what has been going on?'

'Maybe you should explain how things look from your perspective.'

Ursula suggested going for coffee, but Eleanor invited them into the school. In her classroom, the woman prepared three cups of coffee from a cartridge machine on a side bench. She offered milk and sugar.

'I'm sorry, there are no biscuits,' she said.

'This is fine,' Sidney lied. He was dying for something to eat. It had been a long and meagre day cooped up in their van.

Ursula looked around her. The back wall of the classroom held a display of pupils' work. The subject, headlined by large, coloured letters, was the Causeway coast. There were illustrations and notes about its castles and historic characters, but the centrepiece was the story of the *Girona*.

'We do a project every year for my second form class,' Eleanor explained, when Ursula had wandered off to study the display.

'Very impressive,' Ursula said. 'It looks really detailed.' She read the handwritten legends surrounding the huge picture of the ship that had been drawn and painted by pupils.

'It's an important piece of our local history,' said Eleanor. 'The children enjoy hearing the stories. Every year we visit the Girona exhibition at the Ulster Museum. And, of course, we make several trips to the Causeway itself. We visit Dunluce Castle and, weather permitting, we cross the bridge to Carrick-a-Rede. Did you know that it means a rock in the road? It was said to be an obstacle for salmon returning to the mouth of the river where their lives had begun. On a fine day, it's my favourite place in the world.'

'It certainly makes a good story,' Ursula said, rejoining Eleanor and Sidney at the teacher's desk.

'You said Fiona McCabe was to blame for all the trouble,' said Sidney, getting back to the purpose of their meeting. 'What exactly do you mean?'

'Well, you know about the lottery syndicate, from which, incidentally, I had been excluded. Not that I care about such things.'

'Yes,' Sidney and Ursula answered in unison.

'They won a fortune, you know,' Eleanor continued. 'I believe that at least one of them, but not Fiona, claimed the money before she could.'

'Are you suggesting that Fiona murdered Teddy and Natalie because she believed they had claimed the lottery winnings?' Ursula sounded incredulous.

Eleanor gave a gentle shrug.

'But Fiona ran the syndicate,' Ursula continued. 'Her sister Eve told us that Fiona already had the money and the others in the syndicate, including Eve, were insisting on a share of it.'

Sidney, however, did not look so surprised.

'That could explain why Fiona has remained in the area,' he said. 'She's been trying to get her hands on the winnings and has killed in her attempt.'

'That means Eve McCabe lied to us again, Daddy. And it explains why Fiona refused to tell us anything.'

'You've met Fiona?' Eleanor asked, grasping again at the pendant around her neck.

Sidney and Ursula didn't reply and merely gazed at the shocked expression engulfing the woman's face.

'But you must tell the police, Mr Valentine! You must tell Pamela. She has been searching everywhere for her.'

'She's not very good at it, if you ask me,' said Ursula. 'We found Fiona without much trouble.'

Sidney continued to look bewildered.

'I can't believe that Eve has lied to us again,' he said, more to himself than anyone else.

Chapter 45

Since DI Kelso had at least tolerated their presence when they'd met outside the high school earlier in the day, Sidney and Ursula saw no reason to secrete themselves away from the Causeway coast. They booked rooms once again at the Armada Hotel in Bushmills. Further attempts to find a hotel where Fiona might be hiding had so far come to nothing. But from what Eleanor Martinez had told them, it seemed likely that Fiona would not venture far away from Finn Close. Of course, in a small country such as Northern Ireland, 'not far away' could well mean Belfast, only sixty miles to the south. Sidney, despite having lost Fiona, was also intent on staying around the Causeway area. He believed he still had unfinished business with several of the locals.

Ursula, uncharacteristically, was doing everything her father suggested without argument. Sidney reckoned that her nonchalance was masking a degree of post-traumatic stress arising from her abduction. At times like these, Sidney wished better for the daughter he'd raised on his own. It was never an entirely satisfactory arrangement for her to spend so much time darting about the country with him. She should have a settled life with a husband and a couple of kids, or at least have a regular job where she could spend time with people of her own age, having fun and enjoying life.

This evening, she was struggling to eat her dinner, her thoughts apparently somewhere else.

'I'll get them, you know,' he said. 'Whether they have committed murders or stolen lottery money, I'll still get them for what they did to you.'

Ursula looked more like the little girl he used to walk home from school while having to explain why she didn't have a mummy to look after her.

'It doesn't matter, Daddy,' Ursula said. 'There are more important things to worry about.'

'Surely, you don't mean potholes?'

He'd made her laugh.

'Don't be daft. But two people have been murdered and for what? Lottery money? We have to find the killer.'

'I know, pet. I'm just fed up dealing with liars.'

'Do you think Eleanor Martinez has any reason to lie?' Ursula asked.

'I don't believe she has. She seems to be very strait-laced, although she has certainly acquired plenty of information on what's been going on with her neighbours. I reckon she's a curtain-twitcher. She watches everything that goes on in Finn Close.'

'DI Kelso doesn't appear to have any issues with her. They seemed to be friends.'

Sidney smiled.

'Yes. It must have been a real hoot growing up in their street.'

Ursula resumed eating her steak pie and chips.

'I don't know about you, but I'm whacked,' she said, when she'd set down her knife and fork. 'I won't be long out of my bed.'

'Yes, you will,' said Sidney. 'There's work to do this evening.'

'Ach, Daddy, I've tried all the hotels looking for Fiona.'

'If she's not staying at a hotel, I have an inkling of where she might be.'

'You don't think she's gone home to Finn Close? Surely, even she would think that dangerous.'

'We need to find the real reason why she's been hanging around. If she has won the lottery and is already in possession of the money, why is she still here? Eleanor's take seems to be more plausible, that Fiona is trying to get her hands on winnings that others in the syndicate have taken.'

'But that would not explain why she was held captive by farmer Robinson,' said Ursula.

'We still can't be certain that she was.'

'Or maybe it has nothing at all to do with the blessed lottery.' It felt as though she had said that several times already.

'Let's just go with the lottery angle for now,' said Sidney.

They had coffee, then gathered their coats from their rooms and met outside by the van.

'By the way,' said Sidney as he climbed in, 'did you notice the pendant that Eleanor was wearing this afternoon?'

'I did. She fiddled with it quite a bit.'

'It's just like one I saw at the museum when I went to see the treasure from the *Girona*. Eleanor's must be a reproduction. It's of a winged lizard, known as the Salamander Pendant, and the original probably belonged to one of the noblemen officers on the *Girona*.'

'It was quite pretty.' Ursula started the engine. 'Where are we going?'

'Head for the Causeway.'

Chapter 46

The night sky was clear with a bright moon reflected on a gentle ocean swell. It was of no benefit to Sidney and Ursula who would have preferred to remain unseen in the darkness. Ursula stopped the van at a wide spot in the road close to the car park for the Causeway visitor centre. Sidney had decided against using it. They saw one vehicle nestled in a corner; a couple were perhaps enjoying each other's company.

'What now?' Ursula asked.

'We'll cut across the field,' Sidney explained, getting out.

He zipped up his anorak and pulled a woollen beanie down on his head. There was little of his face exposed. Ursula giggled.

'Would you like some boot polish for your face? Just to complete the look,' she joked.

'None of your nonsense,' he replied. 'And keep your voice down. no need to let her know we're coming.'

Ursula peered over the field where two hundred yards away on the far side lay the cottage that had been home to Teddy McNaughten. She could see a single light from a rear window. It seemed that Sidney's hunch was correct. Fiona McCabe could well be hiding in the home of her late boss.

They skirted the perimeter of the field staying close to the hedge to avoid being noticed.

'What exactly are we going to do if Fiona is hiding here?' Ursula whispered.

Sidney, already out of breath, stopped to explain.

'If Fiona is there, then I want the truth. Either she's already in possession of a fortune or she's determined to get her hands on one.'

'She's hardly likely to confess to murder, though. And she might be armed and dangerous.'

'Shut up. I don't need you complicating matters.' He plodded on.

'So sorry,' Ursula whispered with a giggle.

When they were close to the rear of the cottage, the light from the kitchen cast a glare near the spot where Sidney and Ursula hid behind a gorse bush. They were going to have to dash beyond it and over the lawn to reach the cottage.

'We'll check the front before we go in,' Sidney whispered.

They tiptoed around the edge of the rough garden and stopped by the old shed that Teddy had used as a workshop. Ursula smiled at the expression clouding what she could still see of her father's face.

'Not what you'd expected?' she asked.

'Not really.'

The two of them stared at the collection of vehicles scattered along the drive and into the lane. Ursula recognised the SUV belonging to Cissy and Bertie Robinson. Behind it sat the Volkswagen owned by Julie and Curtis, and alongside was a vehicle she thought might perhaps belong to Fiona. A huge tractor sat in the lane. Ursula shuddered. It had to be that nasty farmer's, Bertie and Cissy's son, or perhaps big Royston was allowed out at night. There were lights on in the living room of the cottage, and several figures were visible through the thin curtain.

'What do we do now?' she asked.

'I'm thinking,' Sidney muttered.

Chapter 47

Sidney slid into his seat in the van but, still breathing hard, uttered little except to suggest that they should leave quickly.

Ursula understood Sidney's reluctance to hang around Teddy's cottage because they had no understanding of the situation. Farmer Robinson had held her prisoner once and Sidney had sampled threatening treatment in Eugene's home. It would not be wise to irritate these people any further. If they had already killed Teddy and Natalie, then they wouldn't baulk at killing two more. They attempted to eavesdrop by the lounge window for a few moments, but the voices inside the house were muffled, and they learned nothing. Before leaving, Sidney and Ursula couldn't resist making a small gesture.

'It's just to let them know we were there,' Sidney explained as he caught his breath. 'I'm sure they'll guess it was us. But it's a little payback for what they did to you.'

'Jeepers, Daddy, you sound as if you've just torched the house with them inside. We've only let their tyres down.'

'Well, they had it coming.'

Ursula drove them away, giving the accelerator pedal an extra squeeze just to help shake off her adrenalin.

'We are going to have to confront them at some point,' she said.

'I know, but the time and place will be of our choosing.'

'Do you think we should tell DI Kelso about it?'

'Tell her what exactly? We still can't prove a thing.'

Sidney shot forward as the van braked sharply to a halt on the lane.

'What the hell, Ursula?'

'What if those guys are there right now intending to kill Fiona, to get their hands on the money? And we've done nothing to help her.'

Sidney shook his head at his daughter's outburst. 'Calm down, love. It didn't sound as though a row was going on. Besides, killers don't turn up and park nicely to do away with someone. I would guess, if Fiona was present, that they are there by mutual agreement.'

'In that case, I have no idea what is going on,' she said.

They returned to their hotel and a welcome drink in the bar. Ursula had a pint of Guinness, but Sidney opted for the hard stuff again – a large single malt.

'Where do we go from here?' Ursula asked, sounding disconsolate. 'We can't trust anyone. Apart from Fiona, we don't even have a decent suspect. And besides, we didn't start out to investigate two murders. We were only asked to find Fiona and now we've done that twice perhaps, but so what? The woman doesn't want to be found, at least not by her sister.'

Sidney couldn't disagree. They were working on their own time without pay, and yet he didn't feel inclined to pack it in. There was a principle involved. He had been threatened, and Ursula had been abducted. For whatever reason, he wasn't going to let that go without further recourse.

'Daddy? Are you still with me?'

'There's something going on here,' he replied.

Ursula spluttered her sip of beer.

'Really? Is that it? Is that your big thought?'

'Calm down, Ursula. I'm just thinking out loud. Unless you have any bright ideas, I'm going to my bed. We'll make a fresh start in the morning.'

'Well, I might have something new, but I suppose it can wait till then.'

Ursula bid her father goodnight and sat on in the bar until she'd finished her pint. She half expected one or more of the residents of Finn Close to storm in looking for her and Sidney. They must surely have realised who had interfered with their tyres. She wouldn't sleep tonight wondering why they had gathered at Teddy McNaughten's cottage. She and Sidney had assumed that they were meeting with Fiona. Yet, except for an unidentified car parked in the lane that might belong to the elusive woman, they couldn't be certain that Fiona was even present.

* * *

Next morning, Ursula revealed to Sidney over breakfast new information she had acquired before going to bed. On hearing it, he wolfed down his food and tried to get Ursula to do the same.

'I don't know what the big rush is,' she said, buttering another slice of toast. 'You haven't even told me where we're going or what we're doing.'

'Just hurry up and you'll soon find out. From what you've just told me, you should be able to guess where we're going.'

When eventually they reached the van, Sidney directed Ursula out of town onto Causeway Road, driving beyond Teddy McNaughten's cottage and Finn Close. Despite the new information she'd explained to Sidney, she still did not expect to be turning left into the lane that led to the Robinson farm. She couldn't find the right question to ask; there were so many. Sidney remained quiet and allowed Ursula to drive all the way into the farmyard.

'Prepare yourself,' he warned. 'This might get nasty.'

They got out of the van in time to be faced by an intrigued stare from the big farmer standing by his kitchen door. The silent Royston appeared from a shed next to the house and stood beside his father.

'Morning,' said Sidney.

'It is that,' Robinson replied, his hands shoved deep into his overalls. 'Is there something I can do for you?'

It was just the question Sidney needed to get started. He'd expected a threat and an order to clear off. But a question, he could handle.

'I think we're both happy to admit that it was a clever stunt you pulled the other day for DI Kelso's benefit,' said Sidney.

'Are we now? And what about the one you pulled last night, letting down people's tyres?'

'Call it quits, shall we?'

'Like I said, is there something I can do for you?'

'I think it's about time that people round here were honest with us,' said Sidney. 'After all, we are only doing the job we were hired to do.'

'And what would that be?' said Robinson, his smirk widening.

'Eve McCabe employed us to find her sister Fiona.'

'That's got nothing to do with me.'

'I think it has,' said Sidney. 'You held her here as a prisoner just as you did with Ursula. And I would guess you were meeting with her last night at Teddy's cottage.'

'So what? The police didn't believe a word you told them. Your wee girl was mistaken.'

'I don't think so,' said Ursula.

'You can't prove a thing,' Robinson scoffed. 'Kelso believed me, not you, missy.'

'Oh, I think we can,' said Sidney. 'Isn't that right, Royston?'

The youth seemed confused and looked at his father for guidance.

'No point asking him. He doesn't speak,' said Robinson.

'But he knows how to use a mobile phone,' said Sidney.

'What are you talking about?'

'When you held Ursula here against her will, Royston snatched her phone and didn't return it.'

'Don't know what you're on about. The girl wasn't held prisoner, so how could the boy have her phone?'

'Ursula, call your phone,' said Sidney.

Ursula, with her new phone and new number called her old one. Seconds later, pleasant chimes could be heard in the yard, and Royston gripped at the pocket of his overalls in a futile attempt to stop the noise.

'Doesn't prove a thing,' said Robinson. 'The boy found a phone lying in the lane, that's all.'

'Maybe you should ask him who he's been texting for the past two days,' said Ursula.

She smiled at the big lad who, for the first time in years, seemed on the verge of spluttering a reply.

'Yes, Royston baby, I'm your new friend Laetitia from up the road in Limavady. Nice pictures, by the way. Love your six-pack. Sorry, but my daddy wouldn't let me return the favour. It was cool though, hearing all about the women you've had in those glamping pods. They liked to be tied up, you said.'

Royston looked helpless. His father shook his head.

'Go and see to the calves, boy,' he commanded.

Royston hurried away across the yard. Ursula pressed 'call' again, and the youth jumped when the phone rang in his pocket.

'He said a lot more in our wee chats,' said Ursula. 'Told me all about moving the pods to one of your sheds on the other side of the lane. He also told me how Fiona gave him a lovely shiner as a souvenir before running away. I think the police might be more interested this time.'

'Maybe we can have that wee chat now,' said Sidney.

Robinson rubbed at his face and puffed his cheeks.

'What do you want to know?'

Chapter 48

'Boyso!' Robinson said with a hearty laugh. 'The lottery? Who told you that?'

'Cissy, your mother, started it,' said Ursula. 'She told me that Fiona had gone and taken the money with her.'

'That was just Mammy getting ahead of herself,' said the farmer, still chuckling.

'Then you'd better tell us what's been going on,' said Sidney. 'I'm warning you. Feed us with a pack of lies and we go to the police and tell them about your perverted son.'

Robinson invited them indoors for a cup of tea. Ursula was reluctant, recalling that on her first visit she had probably been drugged as she drank from one of the blue-and-white mugs. Sidney was, as usual, grateful for refreshment and a sit-down. At last, it seemed that matters were about to be resolved quite amicably. When they were seated around the table in the kitchen with mugs of strong tea and a plate of chocolate digestives on offer, Robinson began his story.

'I'll start by telling you that nobody round here has won the lottery, not the jackpot anyway. Boyso, that would be a story right enough.'

'Fiona's sister Eve has also mentioned a lottery win,' said Sidney. 'As did several other residents of Finn Close.'

'I think maybe Fiona has spread that story to distract a few folks.'

'You'd best just tell us your version of events and we can make up our own mind,' said Ursula, frustrated by the growing list of peculiar stories.

'Teddy McNaughten was certain he'd found the *Girona* treasure,' said Robinson.

Sidney rubbed his eyes. Here they go again. Round in circles. First lottery, then treasure, then the lottery and back to treasure. Why couldn't it be a question of adultery, a crime of passion, or even a dispute over the erection of a garden fence?

'So, where is this treasure?' Sidney asked, although he had little enthusiasm for hearing the answer.

'We don't know,' Robinson said with a smile. 'Poor Teddy has taken the secret to his grave.'

'He didn't tell anyone?' Ursula asked.

'At first, we thought he'd told Fiona, but she claimed that Teddy had merely said that he suspected there was treasure somewhere around Finn Close. He didn't say where it was or who had it.'

'You mean, one of the residents has it?' Sidney asked.

'No one is admitting to having it. Fiona had been spooked by the whole thing, you see. Somebody was sending her threatening messages on her phone. My mother suggested she come and stay here on the farm. When Teddy was killed, she started blaming the rest of us, so I kept her here for her own safety, you understand. But the lass wasn't happy, and one night she thumped Royston and took off.'

'Why were you meeting Fiona at Teddy's cottage last night?' said Ursula.

'Boyso, the lass wasn't there. We had been waiting until the police had finished their snooping then we went looking around Teddy's place for clues about the treasure.'

'Was Natalie MacDonnell aware of the treasure?' Sidney asked.

Robinson shook his head and drank some of his tea.

'If she was, she never mentioned it to us.'

'Then why was she killed?' Ursula asked.

Robinson's face flushed instantly. 'Hold on a minute, you don't think that we had anything to do with these murders, do you?'

'You're the ones searching for treasure that Teddy had claimed to know existed,' said Sidney. 'You held Fiona and Ursula here as prisoners. It's hard not to regard you as suspects.'

'When you put it like that, I suppose it's understandable, but I can assure you that we had nothing to do with killing.'

'Can the same be said for all the residents of Finn Close?' said Sidney, rising from his seat. He'd had enough of the fatuous conversation.

As they returned to their van, Royston was strolling across the yard.

'Hey, Royston!' Ursula called. 'Are you ever going to return my phone?'

The youth, looking shifty, dropped his gaze and hurried on.

'That's a no then? Well, don't expect any more sexy texts from me. We're finished, lover boy! No more dick pics, understand?'

She called her old phone again and Royston struggled to pull it from his pocket as it rang. It seemed he hadn't learned his lesson from the last time. Ursula jeered as he scurried across the yard.

* * *

Sidney fancied a walk to clear his head. Ursula drove them to the Causeway car park, and they braved a cool breeze to stroll down the path to the seashore. When they reached the Causeway, father and daughter thought the same thing and ventured onto the array of honeycombed rocks, wondering if perhaps they might find something to do with Natalie. Nothing was so obvious as they peered over the crust of coloured lichen where the rocks met the sea. Ursula studied an outcrop of rock on the opposite side of the bay, known as the Giant's Granny, a formation supposedly resembling a stooped old lady. Ursula was unconvinced. They continued beyond the Causeway and finally halted at the Port Reostan viewpoint. A portion of the cliff face had collapsed years ago, and the path was closed at this point. For a few minutes, they gazed across the bay towards Lacada Point. A short way off, beneath the ocean, lay the wreck of the *Girona.*

'Did you believe Robinson?' Ursula asked Sidney, who had been rather pensive during their walk.

'Not a word,' he replied. 'They're all lying to us. I can't believe they would have been prepared to kill two people over a few gold coins.'

'What about the lottery?'

'More likely, if we're talking a few million quid. But why hasn't it all been settled by now? If Fiona is the recipient of a fortune, why has she been hanging around allowing herself to be hounded by the others? I reckon she was at Teddy's cottage last night and that was her car parked in the lane. But something still irks me about the twin sister thing. I wouldn't trust either one.'

They started to walk back to the van, taking the Shepherd's Steps that led to the clifftop path.

'I have an idea,' said Ursula with an impish smile.

Chapter 49

The following morning, Ursula insisted that Sidney remain in the hotel. She ordered him to have a quiet day, to read the papers, drink coffee and have a wee think about the case that continued to frustrate them. Sidney didn't need much coaxing, although he insisted that Ursula assure him that she would not be placing herself in danger. After breakfast, she dressed in the most fetching clothes she had brought from home: slim jeans, a low-cut jumper and heeled ankle boots. She applied make-up and over-squirted Opium to the extent that anyone would smell her long before she'd even stepped out of her van.

She'd spent the previous evening renewing contact with the gullible young man who was still in possession of her old phone. Despite her last words to him in the farmyard when she'd joked that their relationship was over, it didn't take long to re-engage. Several juicy texts and a picture of her in pyjamas was sufficient for Royston to return a series of images featuring a cherished portion of his anatomy. The net result of the exchange was a morning rendezvous at the harbour in Ballintoy.

She made sure that she got there before the arranged time. It was the place where Ursula had been released by Robinson, a car park by a neat harbour nestled beneath chalk cliffs. Two stone lime kilns stood to one side, reminders of its past function in exporting lime. Nowadays, with its winding road descending to the harbour, picturesque church and architecturally eccentric Bendhu House, Ballintoy was more likely to be a setting for a movie. Thankfully, this morning it was deserted.

When the big tractor rolled into the car park, Ursula was leaning on the bonnet of the van, her brown hair swept back, and anorak open to show off her large bosom. At least in the fresh air the whiff of her perfume would not be so intense. She smiled and pouted as Royston climbed down from the cab of his tractor.

'Morning, babe,' she said, maintaining her pose. His eyes were tracing her up and down before settling on her most prominent of features. 'I brought you a wee prezzie.'

His eyes widened but, of course, he didn't manage to speak. Ursula passed him a packet of chocolate digestives and proffered a thermos of tea.

'Must be time for a big strapping farmer to have a wee break.' She strutted around her van, reached the passenger door and opened it wide. 'You'll be more comfortable in here.'

With his biscuits in one hand and flask in the other, Royston and his big wellies plodded over and sat in the van. Ursula leaned in, just enough for her guest to get a good view.

'Make yourself comfortable,' she whispered. 'No need for seatbelts.' She blew him a kiss then slammed his door and paraded around the bonnet until she climbed in behind the wheel. She turned towards him and smiled.

Royston already looked out of his depth, still holding biscuits and thermos.

'Will I take that?' she said, relieving him of the flask. 'You eat your biscuits and I'll be mummy.'

She slipped the cup from the top of the flask, removed the cap and poured some tea. There was little response from the young farmer, but Ursula was hoping she might be able to get the first words out of him in years. She just had to take things slowly. She handed him the cup of tea.

'I hope you like it strong and sweet,' she said, stroking the back of his head. 'Do you know you have beautiful eyes?'

Royston shifted in his seat as he stuffed biscuits into his mouth and slurped his tea. Ursula maintained her smile and kept her cleavage on show.

'I know you don't say much, Royston, but you can talk to me, you know. No need to be frightened of me, is there? Thanks for the pictures, by the way. Did you like the one I sent you?'

He nodded and wiped his mouth with the back of his hand.

Ursula took the plastic cup from him and hoped that he wouldn't stuff another biscuit in his mouth.

'I can send you lots more, but you have to do something for me,' she whispered in his ear. She heard a grunt and felt a hand on her leg and drew back.

'What does a big farmer boy get up to when he's not feeding the cows or taking wee pictures of himself to send to all his girlfriends?'

'Don't.'

It was barely audible, but Ursula was sure he'd said a word. Suddenly, there was a hand firmly on her right breast, squeezing, weighing and pressing.

'What did you say, Royston?'

Stealthily, she swiped his big hand away.

'I-I don't have girlfriends.'

Ursula smiled warmly, a little sympathy welling inside her. She had an ulterior motive, but at least she had him talking.

'Wow! Is this the first time you've said anything since poor Jodie was killed?'

'Not really. I just don't talk to me mammy and daddy. But I talk to myself.'

'But that's great, Royston.'

She leaned over and gave him a hug. He tried to fondle her breast again, but she pushed his hand away.

'Enough of that for now; you'll be getting me all excited. I just want to hear you talk. Tell me all about yourself.'

'Not much to say.'

'I'm sure that's not true. I'll bet you've been dying to talk to someone like me.' She raised his chin with her hand to divert his eyes from her cleavage. 'Tell me about yourself.'

'I get fed up working on the farm all the time. My father tells me that one day it will be mine to look after, but I don't want it. It's a lonely job. I have no mates and it's impossible to find a girlfriend. I just want to get away from here to the city and become a plumber. I hear they make loads of money.'

Ursula smiled sympathetically.

'How do you get on with Cissy and Bertie?'

'All right, I suppose. I don't talk to them either. I don't bother talking to anyone who thinks I'm just my father's daft son.'

'So, what's happening with your grandparents and their neighbours?'

His gaze settled again on her cleavage. She was fighting a losing battle, but if he was comfortable, she thought, he might be more forthcoming with information.

'There's been a big argument,' he said, crunching another biscuit.

'With Fiona?'

'Aye.'

'What are they arguing about?'

'Money. They won the lottery.'

'So, it's not about treasure from the *Girona*?'

Royston shook his head and looked as though she'd just asked a daft question.

'Did they kill Teddy and Natalie over lottery money?'

Royston shrugged.

Chapter 50

Sidney was in his room at the Armada when Ursula returned from her liaison with Royston. He opened the door to her knock, then moved back inside, too engrossed in what he was doing to even speak. Ursula smiled in amusement when she gazed at his work.

'You do know that it's a popular myth?' she said.

'What is?'

'Detectives, police or otherwise, do not stick wee notes all over the wall, stare at them for days then suddenly come up with the solution to their case. It doesn't work like that.'

She threw herself on his bed and, sprawled over two pillows, watched as Sidney continued to arrange several dozen Post-it notes on the blank wall to the left of the dressing table.

'Royston has just told me that the whole thing is about the lottery,' she said. She'd expected her father to stop and listen, but he continued with his project. 'His da fed us more lies. It's got nothing to do with *Girona* treasure.'

Still nothing from Sidney.

'Daddy!'

'Right,' he said, but hardly in response to Ursula's shout. 'Listen to this.'

He stood as if he was a college lecturer about to enrich the minds of his students. He swept a hand over his morning's work.

'I've arranged everything we know so far and placed it under the names of the relevant suspects.'

There was a column for each resident of Finn Close, plus farmer Robinson, Eve and DI Kelso. Background information on the murder victims Teddy McNaughten and Natalie MacDonnell was also displayed.

Ursula had something to tell him, but Sidney was in single-track mode, and she thought it best just to let him continue.

'There is one thing that links all of the residents,' said Sidney. His eyes fixed to the information on the wall. 'The *Girona*.'

'What do you mean?'

'Well, every house in that cul-de-sac has a picture of the ship in their homes. Bertie has a scale model. Eleanor was wearing a reproduction of the Salamander Pendant the other day, and she teaches her students about the *Girona* story. Teddy was obsessed with finding treasure that was supposedly taken from the ship at the time it sank.'

'We didn't find anything about the *Girona* in Natalie's house,' said Ursula.

Sidney frowned; his little theory dashed.

'Now, can I tell you what I found out from Royston?'

'Royston? Is that why you're done up to the nines and smelling like a tart's boudoir?'

'Thanks very much. Nice one, Daddy.' She sat up on the bed. 'Just be quiet and listen.'

Looking dejected, Sidney slumped into the only armchair in the room while continuing to scan his notes on the wall.

'I'm all ears,' he said.

'Firstly, Royston can speak. He told me lots of things.'

'But do I, as your father, want to hear them?'

'He is adamant that the syndicate won the lottery. They just have one tiny problem.'

'Which is?'

'They're a pack of dinosaurs.'

Sidney looked blank and waited for Ursula to elaborate.

'You'd think in this day and age that everyone who plays the lottery does it online,' she said with a snigger. 'They choose their numbers and make payments on the lottery website. Everything is automated and you can even pay by direct debit so that you never miss a draw. But not the folks at Finn Close. They were still buying tickets at a shop in Bushmills every week.'

'So?'

'They all reckon they've won, but they can't find the winning ticket.'

Chapter 51

'It seems that they're blaming each other,' said Ursula. 'They started by accusing Fiona of having it, since she ran their syndicate. That's why they held her prisoner and ransacked her house. They feared she was about to do a runner with the winning ticket. Eve hired us to find Fiona when she couldn't contact her, also fearing that her sister had fled. According to Royston, Fiona insists that Teddy had the winning ticket. She claimed that Teddy had placed the syndicate's entry for the week when they supposedly won. Apparently, he'd volunteered because he was going to the shop in Bushmills after work one afternoon when Fiona still had a tour group to show around the Causeway. After the lottery draw that weekend, Teddy, apparently, didn't get around to checking their numbers.'

'We were told previously that they used different numbers every week,' said Sidney. 'So how did any of them know that they'd won?'

'Well,' Ursula continued, 'a rumour was circulating that a winning jackpot ticket had been bought in the north Antrim area and the prize had not been claimed. That's when the others came after Fiona, accusing her of trying to keep the money for herself. She denied it, of course, and reminded Teddy that if he couldn't be bothered checking their numbers, he should hand over the ticket. Before he could do that, Fiona was imprisoned on the Robinson farm. Then Teddy was murdered.'

Sidney jumped up and cast his eyes over his evidence wall.

'So, we might not have had events in the correct order,' he said, 'but we still have the same suspects for the murders of Teddy and Natalie.'

'Royston's story explains why Fiona hasn't tried to leave the area,' Ursula continued. 'She and the others are searching for a winning lottery ticket. It explains why we found Fiona's house in a mess. One or more of the others had been searching for the ticket. That's also why they were at Teddy's cottage the other night. As we suspected, Fiona was there too.'

'And two people are already dead because of it.' Sidney sighed. Then he turned to Ursula, his expression again full of doubt.

Ursula realised that little had been achieved if they couldn't find proof.

'Given that everyone in Finn Close has lied their face off,' said Sidney, 'what makes you believe that Royston is telling the truth?'

Ursula cleared her throat then wafted a hand over her face.

'I may have had an effect on the poor lad,' she said. 'I don't think he would lie to me. He overdosed on my perfume.'

Sidney rolled his eyes, but his attention returned to his notes on the wall. He began to rearrange several of them.

'If, and it's a big if, young Royston has been straight with you, then the *Girona* treasure can be discounted as a motive, and Eleanor Martinez can also be removed as a suspect since she was not a member of the lottery syndicate.' He removed the Post-its under Eleanor's name and all references to the *Girona*. 'As far as the syndicate members are concerned, my money is still on Fiona McCabe as our killer.'

'No one has proved that the syndicate had a winning ticket,' said Ursula. 'Royston didn't know for certain. According to him, no ticket has been found. We don't know for sure whether Teddy ever got around to checking the numbers, or if he even placed the entry for that week. If Fiona had got her hands on a winning ticket, whether she'd killed to get it or not, she wouldn't still be here.'

'So, where is it?'

Sidney examined his wall.

'The answer isn't up there, Daddy.'

'There's one thing still puzzling me,' he said. 'If Teddy was killed by someone trying to get their hands on the winning lottery ticket, why was Natalie murdered?'

'Maybe the killer suspected Natalie of having it, especially if Teddy and Natalie were lovers.'

'That suggests that the killer isn't bothered who dies as long as they find the ticket. But if they're still searching for it, why haven't there been further murders?'

Ursula shuddered at the thought. She'd been held as a prisoner for merely wandering onto the Robinson farm. It might have spelt her end and yet she'd been released a day later. Such action didn't point towards the Robinsons being the killers. Royston had told her she had been released because Fiona had escaped the night before, after smashing a plate on his head and punching him in the eye. They'd been worried that she would bring the police to the farm. With no one being held there and the pods moved out of sight, it was easy to deny the whole thing to DI Kelso.

'I think we can discount the Robinson family,' said Ursula. 'They had Fiona, and they had me. If they were killers, why not kill us?'

'Fair enough,' Sidney replied, removing all references to the Robinsons from the wall. 'That leaves Eugene, Curtis and Julie, and Fiona.'

'You can remove Fiona's name too,' said Ursula.

'But she's still my number-one suspect.'

'At the time Teddy was murdered, she was being held prisoner by Robinson.'

'And then there were three.'

Sidney peeled off the notes below Fiona's name. Father and daughter stared glumly at the remaining suspects.

'What were you saying about getting answers from an evidence wall?' Sidney said.

'You still haven't.'

'Then we need to take a closer look at Eugene, and Curtis and Julie.'

Chapter 52

One aspect of the murder investigation that Sidney and Ursula had not yet accomplished was that of asking each suspect to establish their alibi for the time when Teddy McNaughten had been murdered. But father and daughter were not police officers; they were not privy to the details of the victim's exact time of death. They only had their own estimation to rely on. As for the second victim, Natalie MacDonnell, an accurate time of death, even for police with access to forensic analysis, could not be established. Natalie's body had been washed ashore on the Giant's Causeway. No one, except the killer, knew exactly where and when she had entered the sea. Natalie may have been killed before Teddy, at the same time, or afterwards. In Natalie's case, alibis extracted from suspects would mean little.

Following their intense deliberations of the previous day, Sidney and Ursula were now focussing their investigation upon Eugene the postman, and Curtis and Julie. Asking any of these people to account for their whereabouts around the time that Teddy was murdered was unlikely to yield truthful responses. The alternative was to ask the one person who didn't get involved in the social activities of Finn Close but who seemed to know about everything that occurred in the cul-de-sac.

Eleanor Martinez seemed uneasy at being greeted by the father and daughter detectives on her doorstep.

It was raining heavily and, while Ursula had at least worn a hooded anorak, Sidney's woollen jumper was soaking and sagged on his shoulders.

'You'd better come in,' said Eleanor, with little warmth in her voice. 'I'm just about to leave for work.'

'That's why we called early,' Sidney explained. 'Thought we'd catch you before you left.'

They remained in the hallway of the bungalow as Eleanor retrieved her coat from a cloakroom.

'Can you recall seeing Eugene, Curtis and Julie in the close around the time Teddy McNaughten was murdered?'

'Gosh,' she said, pulling on her coat and stooping for her handbag. 'I'd have to think for a moment. When was that exactly?'

'We found Teddy's body two Saturdays ago,' said Ursula, 'but we can't be sure of the day he was killed. Possibly three or four days before then.'

'I see,' said Eleanor, now looking eager to leave for work. She shook her head. 'Sorry, I can't think of anything in relation to those people,' she said. 'I see a lot of coming and going but nothing registers as being strange. Eugene keeps odd hours, but he is a postman. I do recall seeing Curtis and Julie chatting with Natalie beside her car around that time, I suppose. Yes, of course, I was returning to school for a parents' evening on the Tuesday before Teddy was found. I saw the three of them as I was leaving. They didn't acknowledge me but then they never do.'

'Did you see Teddy in the close during that week?' Sidney asked.

Eleanor moved toward her door. Sidney realised they were holding her back and stepped outside.

'No. I definitely did not see Teddy.'

'Well, thanks anyway, Eleanor,' said Sidney.

The woman closed her front door behind them and hurried to her car.

'Why are you asking about Eugene, and Curtis and Julie?' she said. 'I thought that you'd already found Fiona.'

'Just trying to clear up a few loose ends,' Sidney replied.

'Do you know?' Eleanor said, pausing by her car door. 'I do remember one instance that I considered a bit odd.'

'What's that?' Sidney asked.

'During that week, before Teddy died, I noticed a stranger in the close.'

'A stranger you say?'

'Well, he wasn't a regular visitor in the close, but I did recognise him. It was Natalie's ex-husband. He owns a shop in Coleraine. He's quite well known in the area.'

'Where did he go in the close?'

'To Natalie's, of course.'

Chapter 53

They sat in their van, parked on Main Street in Bushmills, waiting to spy the postman on his rounds. Sidney thought it best to tackle Eugene away from Finn Close to prevent another show of solidarity by Curtis and Bertie in defence of their neighbour. Ursula spotted him first and was out of the van before Sidney even managed to open his door.

'Hey, Eugene!' she called, jogging towards him.

The postman stopped in his tracks and scowled. Ursula guessed he was weighing up his options. He could run, duck into a shop, or stand and face her. It looked as though he'd decided to confront her, but then he noticed Sidney approaching and hurried into a charity shop.

'I'll go round the back in case he tries to escape that way,' said Ursula.

Sidney nodded and proceeded into the shop.

Ursula ran forty yards along the street then turned left into an alley that she hoped would give her access to the rear of the charity shop. When she turned left again, the alley opened out behind the terrace of shops and private houses. On her right, was an area of rough ground and several gardens. It was no surprise for Ursula to see the hapless Eugene emerge from the rear of the shop and turn towards her. Realising his mistake, he darted sideways into a poorly maintained garden that was bordered by a stone wall about four feet high.

'Ach, Eugene!' she called. 'I only want to talk to you.'

She ran after him. Entering the garden, she watched in amusement as Eugene, struggling with his postbag, tried to scale the ivy-clad wall. Ursula folded her arms and giggled at his wretched display of clumsiness. The young man had poor physical ability. He was never going to make it over the wall. Ursula could have sworn she heard him whimper.

'Will you stop for a minute?' she said. 'I just want to ask you a couple of questions.'

Sidney arrived and it sparked further panic in Eugene.

'You stay away from me!' Eugene said. 'Bertie told you to leave me alone.' He tried again to climb over the wall.

'Give it up, Eugene love. You'll do yourself an injury,' said Ursula. 'We only want to know when you last had contact with Teddy.'

Eugene halted his grappling; his face was flushed.

'I didn't.'

'Didn't what?' Ursula asked.

'I didn't really know Teddy. Not well. I didn't see him the night he was killed.'

'What night was that?'

Eugene looked puzzled. Seldom had Ursula met someone who expressed so many thoughts and emotions at the same time.

'I don't understand,' he said nervously.

'You said you never saw Teddy the night he was killed; what night was that?'

'I don't know.'

'OK, so what were you doing that night?' said Ursula, battling with her patience.

'I was at home. I had to be up early for work.'

'Did you see anything strange around the close that night?'

'What night?'

'For flip's sake, Eugene. You're not making this easy. On the night that you didn't know that Teddy was killed, did you see anybody acting suspiciously in the close?'

'I don't think so,' he replied.

'What about when you were getting up early to go to work? Did you see anyone then?'

Ursula studied the man's vague look. It was as if his thoughts had gripped his face and were pulling and twisting at his skin. But she guessed that something was stirring.

'Who did you see, Eugene?' she asked.

He looked directly at her then seemed agitated again by Sidney's presence.

'Why do you need to know? You said you were looking for Fiona.'

'Who did you see, Eugene? It's important,' said Ursula.

'It's got nothing to do with Fiona. Go away. Leave me alone.' He resumed his attempt to conquer the garden wall, slipped and grazed his leg. 'Ow! Just leave me alone,' he cried.

'Who was it, Eugene?' Ursula persisted.

'Natalie. I saw Natalie.'

'What was she doing?'

'She was packing stuff in her car.'

'See anyone else?'

'Just Natalie. Now clear off!'

Ursula and Sidney strolled away, leaving Eugene to decide whether to continue his attempt on the wall or simply return to Main Street and carry on delivering the mail.

'What do you think?' Sidney asked. 'Is Eugene our killer?'

'Don't be daft, Daddy. The man can't even climb a four-foot wall. How's he going to murder anybody?'

They left the van where it was and walked back to their hotel at the far end of Main Street beyond the war memorial. Following the chase, Sidney reckoned he was overdue a coffee break.

'That's one thing we haven't considered,' he said, buttering a fruit scone. 'That Natalie murdered Teddy and then took her own life.'

'But who commits suicide with an antique sword and then jumps into the sea?'

'Not impossible.'

'Stop it, Daddy. Now you're talking nonsense. And you do realise that if we're discounting Eugene as the killer, we're only left with Curtis and Julie?'

'We should ask them what they were discussing with Natalie when Eleanor saw them in the close.'

It was Ursula's face that suddenly contorted in thought and Sidney noticed.

'What?' he said.

'We do have another suspect,' said Ursula. 'Eleanor told us that she'd seen Natalie's ex-husband in Finn Close.'

'Of course! That's it,' Sidney jeered. 'These murders have nothing to do with winning the lottery or finding Spanish treasure. And they have no connection to Fiona McCabe disappearing. MacDonnell found out his ex-wife had been seeing Teddy McNaughten, and he killed them both.'

'Or maybe he heard about the lottery win and killed them to get his hands on the winning ticket?' said Ursula.

'Bloody lottery won't leave us alone, will it?'

Chapter 54

Surveillance of Curtis and Julie was a little trickier than confronting a hapless postman because it was likely the couple had separate jobs in different locations. Once again,

Sidney and Ursula wished to avoid a confrontation at Finn Close where Bertie Robinson might be a threat to any conversation. They didn't know, however, where Julie spent her days. When Ursula had been following her previously, the last she'd seen of the woman was her driving away from the Robinson farm. Ursula surmised that Julie had probably been delivering food to Fiona, who at that time was held captive in a glamping pod. With no tabs on Julie, Sidney and Ursula sat in their van close to the joinery works where they believed Curtis was employed. They began their stake-out at four o'clock, guessing that the young man would probably finish his day's work sometime after then. They hoped also that Julie would arrive to collect her partner.

At 4.25 the Volkswagen with Julie behind the wheel stopped across the entrance to the joinery works. Sidney and Ursula had a choice. They could either speak to Julie while she waited for Curtis, or they could catch the couple together when Curtis emerged from the building. Ursula felt a nudge from Sidney.

'Let's go,' he said.

She was about to get out of the van, but Sidney stopped her.

'Move a bit closer,' he said.

Ursula started the engine and rolled forward, coming to a halt alongside Julie's car. It was a narrow dead-end street. A lorry belonging to the joinery works was parked in front of the Volkswagen. If Julie attempted to flee, she would be unable to simply drive off. Ursula saw the disgruntled look on the young woman's face when she realised that she'd just been hemmed in by two people she had no desire to see. Sidney remained in the van, allowing Ursula the privilege of greeting the woman they'd just cornered.

Ursula stood by the window of the Volkswagen. Julie looked to be undecided about lowering it. Ursula smiled, an indication that she wasn't going anywhere until Julie agreed to speak to her. Eventually, the window slid downwards.

'What?'

'Just wondered if you have time for a wee chat, Julie?' Ursula asked.

'I can't help you to find Fiona. I don't know where she is.'

'You mean, you don't know where she is since the time when you helped to keep her a prisoner on the Robinson farm?'

'I don't know what you're talking about,' said Julie.

'Doesn't matter,' said Ursula. 'Just tell me what you and Curtis were discussing with Natalie shortly before she was murdered.'

'What? We had nothing to do with Natalie's death.'

'I haven't accused you of anything. I just want to know what you discussed when you chatted beside her car in Finn Close.'

Julie seemed puzzled.

'I can't remember,' she replied, shaking her head. 'We were probably talking about the lottery win. Natalie had promised to ask Teddy about our ticket.'

'Was that the last time you saw her?'

Julie shrugged. 'It must have been,' she said.

'And what about Teddy? When did you last see him?'

'Hold on a minute, I don't have to answer your questions. You're not cops. Why don't you clear off and leave us alone?' She raised her window and sat with her arms folded, gazing straight ahead.

Ursula got back into the   van. As she recounted her conversation to Sidney, Curtis emerged from the joinery works and got into the Volkswagen. Immediately, Julie motioned to Ursula, making it clear that she wanted to drive away. Ursula reversed the van, allowing space for the Volkswagen to move off. Julie drove to the end of the street, turned around and came back towards them.

'At least they know we're on to them,' said Sidney.

'The only problem is that I don't think Julie is lying to us,' said Ursula, watching in her mirror as the Volkswagen turned into Main Street and disappeared. 'She was the first person to tell us about the lottery syndicate. At the time when she told us, Teddy and Natalie were already dead. Julie wouldn't have been so forthcoming about a lottery win if she and Curtis had just committed murder over it.'

Sidney rubbed disconsolately at his face.

'Then we're left with this MacDonnell fella,' he said. 'We could draw a blank with him and be home in time for tea.'

'Or, being the last person we think of, he turns out to be our killer.'

* * *

They knew little about Natalie MacDonnell's ex-husband except that his first name was Harry, and he owned a hardware shop in Coleraine. Using her phone, Ursula located the store with Google Maps. She checked that it hadn't yet closed for the evening then drove away from the Dunluce Joinery Works.

MacDonnell's Hardware, Tools and Hire, having for generations stood in Church Street in the heart of the town centre, was nowadays located within a small industrial estate on the ring road. Ursula drove through the gates and stopped in front of the large window of the customer showroom. Sidney did the honours this time and went inside to ask for Harry MacDonnell. He was back in the van a few minutes later.

'Any joy?' Ursula asked.

'He wasn't there, but I got his home address. The assistant called his boss, told him who I am, and surprise, surprise, he agreed to meet us.'

'Very accommodating.'

'Mm. Makes you wonder,' said Sidney. 'If this chap is not involved in this fiasco, then we're done. If he's happy to meet us, does that mean he has nothing to hide?'

Chapter 55

Twenty minutes later, they pulled off the coast road, half a mile from Portstewart, into the paved driveway of an expansive modern house with a commanding sea view. Ursula whistled.

'Obviously, there's money in the hardware trade,' she said. 'This place must be worth a fortune.'

The most prominent feature of the sprawling residence was the enormous glass frontage that extended over two storeys. Sidney noticed a man looking down from the first floor as they got out of the van. A pleasant-looking woman had already opened the front door to greet them.

'Hello,' she chirped. 'Are you Mr Valentine?'

Sidney confirmed that he was and introduced Ursula.

'Nice to meet you, I'm Deirdre. Harry is upstairs in the lounge.'

The woman seemed to be of a similar age to Ursula with long dark hair, a deep tan and the slim physique of a catwalk model. She led them up a chrome-frame staircase into a spacious lounge that gave the impression of being open to the ocean beyond. The man who'd watched them arrive turned from the window.

'Afternoon,' he said in a loud voice that matched his massive frame. Ursula was thinking WWE, Sidney more Giant Haystacks, a wrestling favourite from his youth. 'What can I do you for, Mr Valentine?'

'Please, call me Sidney and this is my daughter Ursula.'

Harry MacDonnell shook hands with them, and Deirdre went off to make coffee. They were invited to sit. The choice of three sofas and several armchairs within the spacious room was baffling. Harry pre-empted their decision by dropping into a wide armchair that still managed to swivel under the man's bulk. Ursula chose a similar seat at the opposite end of a huge marble coffee table. That left Sidney with the vastness of a long corner sofa. Ursula grinned at her father; he looked a little boy lost.

Sidney explained the reason for their visit, about their search for Fiona that had become entangled in the murder of two people and with a supposed lottery win. He was keen to make it seem as though they were still searching for Fiona rather than hunting for a murderer. Harry seemed to listen patiently. Ursula pondered what she already knew of the man. Karen, the barmaid at the Armada Hotel, had said that he had been an abusive husband to Natalie, and that she was best rid of him. His current partner Deirdre, however, appeared friendly and at ease.

'So, how can I help you with this?' Harry asked when Sidney paused in his explanation. 'All I can say is that I was devastated to hear Natalie was dead. We didn't exactly remain friends after we divorced, but I never wanted to see her come to any harm.'

Deirdre returned with a tray of coffee already poured into mugs. At the mention of Natalie, an uncomfortable silence ensued. Understandably, Ursula didn't imagine it to be a popular topic between the pair. The woman handed round the coffee then left without a word. Sidney restarted the conversation.

'We were wondering if you had any contact with Natalie in the days prior to her death?' he asked.

'And just how would that be relevant to your job of finding this Fiona woman?'

It was the first sign that Harry wasn't entirely comfortable with their visit. His mask of gentility, for whatever reason, was beginning to slip.

Sidney reiterated his belief that the reasons surrounding Fiona's disappearance were linked to the murders of

Teddy and Natalie. Harry now seemed to bristle at the subject.

'We believe that you recently visited Finn Close and spoke to your ex-wife,' Sidney continued. 'A few days later, it seems, she was dead.'

'And you think I killed her?'

'I didn't say that. I was just wondering why you'd gone there and what you discussed with Natalie.'

The man glowered at Sidney, his face throbbing and turning puce. Ursula now saw how Harry could be so easily riled and perhaps why Karen had said that Natalie was safer away from him.

'You mentioned the lottery,' said Harry. 'I'd heard the rumours, so I went to ask Natalie if she'd won. Simple as that.'

'And then what?' Sidney asked.

'Well, I wanted to know if there was anything in it for me.'

'Even though you were no longer married?'

Harry shrugged as if to suggest that he still had a say in Natalie's life and a right to her money. Ursula hated his type. She could do nothing for Natalie, but perhaps the woman who'd just served them coffee might need rescuing from such a brute. Sidney wasn't finished.

'What did she tell you?'

'Nothing. Refused to say whether she'd won or not.'

'And was that the last time you saw her?'

'It was, aye. So, don't be thinking I had anything to do with her murder.' Harry got to his feet. It seemed he'd had enough of their conversation.

'I think it's time you and your wee daughter were on your way,' he said brusquely. 'Don't know what I was thinking, allowing you to come here, only to accuse me of murder.'

Sidney and Ursula got to their feet, but Harry still had more to say.

'Tell me this, who told you that I went to see Natalie?'

'That's confidential,' Sidney replied.

'Natalie told me what they're like in Finn Close. Was it that interfering old biddy Cissy Robinson? Can't keep her nose out of other people's business. Or was it that mad cow, the schoolteacher? She threatens everybody with hell and damnation. Nutjob, she is. A religious freak, I'd guess. Maybe it's her you should be accusing.'

Chapter 56

Back at the Armada Hotel, Sidney and Ursula were rather pensive during dinner. Neither father nor daughter was certain of a way forward in their investigation. They'd drifted far from their original task of finding Fiona McCabe. In between, they'd stumbled upon two murders, an apparent lottery-winning syndicate, a quest for Spanish treasure and Ursula had been abducted and held captive for two days. The upshot of their experiences was that none of it made sense, while they were surrounded by people they couldn't trust. Everyone, it seemed, had lied to them.

'Do you know, love. I've had enough of this,' Sidney said, toying with the sirloin steak on his plate.

'We're not giving up now, Daddy.'

'It's not as if we're still getting paid. We found Fiona, but she didn't want her sister to know where she was hiding. Now she's scarpered again. Whatever the reason, it's not our business anymore. We've bumped into a weird bunch of people who deserve each other. Either all of them are guilty of murder or we've missed something. We've eliminated all the suspects.'

'I have one more idea,' said Ursula.

'Of course you have. Let's hear it then. You're not going to let me go home without trying it.'

'You'll just have to wait and see.'

* * *

The next morning, after checking out of the hotel, Ursula drove them to the police station in Coleraine. She asked a nice police constable at the reception desk if she could speak with DI Kelso. Ursula had insisted that Sidney should say nothing. It would only take one word from him to get the detective's back up. An hour passed, and Sidney was fit to be tied.

'She's doing this deliberately, keeping us waiting,' he grumbled.

'She might be genuinely busy,' said Ursula. 'Have some patience.'

'You still haven't told me why we're doing this.'

'I'm thinking that maybe if we share what we know with Kelso, she might reveal something new to us.'

At that moment, the stern face of DI Kelso appeared from a doorway beside the station's reception. It was a given that the detective was less than pleased to see them. If she had been prepared to smile, then the idea was swiftly abandoned when Sidney rose to greet her. Ursula beat him to it.

'DI Kelso, thank you for seeing us,' she said.

'I'm regretting this already, but what can I do for you?' Kelso replied.

'Well,' Ursula began in her most agreeable tone, 'we have more or less finished our work up here, and I thought you might be interested in a few things that we uncovered. It might help with your murder investigation.'

'I doubt that,' said Kelso, 'but let's hear it.'

The detective led them through a doorway to the rear of the station building. They were shown into a windowless room that struck Ursula as being a space for interviewing crime suspects. There was a table, four chairs, an audio and video recording device, and blank walls with a camera mounted high in one corner.

Once they were seated, Ursula ran through the information they had gathered on each resident of Finn Close. She only had to nudge Sidney once to keep him silent.

Kelso shook her head.

'I can't see how any of this helps me,' she said drily.

Ursula was undeterred. She went on to explain about the supposed lottery win and how that remained a mystery since no one seemed to know the whereabouts of a potentially winning ticket.

'It's a clear motive for murder,' said Ursula. 'Especially for the killing of Teddy McNaughten. Since Teddy and Natalie were lovers, it's also a motive for someone to murder Natalie.'

'Lovers?' Kelso's face seemed to light up. 'Who told you they were lovers?'

'We guessed.'

'You guessed? Have you any evidence to support your guess?'

'It was the way Teddy was dressed when we found him,' said Ursula. 'At first, we thought he just liked to dress up as a pirate. Then we realised, since he'd been searching for treasure from the *Girona*, that he was wearing clothes similar to what a Spanish nobleman from the Armada would have worn.'

Kelso looked to be losing patience or her grasp of the plot. Probably both. Ursula ploughed on.

'Teddy had loads of other unusual clothes in his home. When Natalie was found, she was wearing a cone-shaped bra like the one Madonna used to wear. She also kept erotic clothing in her bedroom. We thought that perhaps Teddy and Natalie had engaged in a spot of sexual role playing.'

'How do you know what Natalie was wearing when she was found?' Kelso snapped. 'And what were you doing in her house?'

Ursula winced. She'd messed up. That was not the thing to let slip to this irascible cop. She cleared her throat.

'Not important,' she said bravely. 'The thing is, if they were lovers and they had the winning lottery ticket in their possession, then it was likely they were killed by another member of the syndicate who was trying to claim the money. That's why we at first suspected Fiona McCabe. It's also the reason why Eve McCabe hired us to find Fiona.'

Ursula stopped talking. She watched DI Kelso. A faraway look had developed on the detective's face.

'DI Kelso, are you all right?' Ursula asked.

The woman's face had paled. She stared vacantly into space.

'DI Kelso?' Ursula tried again.

'Sorry,' said Kelso at last. 'Go on with what you were saying.'

Ursula proceeded to explain how they had eliminated each resident of Finn Close from suspicion of the murders.

'We also spoke with Harry MacDonnell, Natalie's ex-husband.'

'Harry? What's he got to do with your search for Fiona McCabe?' Kelso replied, clearly still distracted.

'He was seen talking to Natalie in Finn Close sometime before she was killed. He told us that he'd gone there to find out about the lottery win. He claims that he didn't learn either way if Natalie and the others had won. It is still a motive for killing Natalie, but we have no proof. You might want to interview him.'

A silence ensued, and Ursula was beginning to think that Kelso was feeling unwell. By now the cop should be screaming at them for tramping all over her murder investigation. Instead, she sat resting her chin in her hands, looking far removed from what Ursula was telling her.

Ursula gazed at Sidney. He shrugged. He had no clue as to what was going on. The detective didn't seem to be appreciating the chat.

'Who witnessed Harry MacDonnell talking to Natalie?' Kelso asked. 'No one mentioned it when we conducted house-to-house enquiries.'

'It was Eleanor,' Ursula replied, puzzled by the question. It hardly seemed important now.

Kelso nodded like she understood perfectly.

'I was going to ask you about Eleanor,' said Ursula, 'since you grew up with her and Teddy.'

'Lovers, you say?'

'Teddy and Natalie, yes.' Ursula now felt as confused as Sidney looked.

Kelso suddenly got to her feet, her chair scraping across the floor behind her.

'Sorry, we'll have to leave it there,' she said, making for the door. 'Thank you for the information. It's been very enlightening.' Kelso ushered Sidney and Ursula back through the station reception. 'Have a safe journey home.'

Kelso closed the door behind her, leaving father and daughter looking bewildered.

'What just happened there?' said Sidney. 'Did that woman thank us?'

'She did, aye. Something is up with her, though. I wonder if it was something I said.'

Chapter 57

Although they were packed and ready for the journey home, Sidney and Ursula lingered in their van outside Coleraine police station. Ursula switched on the ignition periodically to get the wipers working. It was raining heavily, and she didn't want their view of the station's entrance to be obscured. They were convinced that DI Kelso would very soon make a speedy exit. Her intended destination was, however, a subject of debate.

'You got the woman thinking about Harry MacDonnell,' said Sidney. 'Although I can't believe she hasn't already suspected him of the murders. You'd think that an ex-husband of one of the victims would be an early port of call for an investigating officer.'

'It seems to me that she hadn't considered the likelihood of Natalie and Teddy being lovers,' said Ursula. 'But perhaps because Teddy's body was discovered first, Kelso wouldn't have considered Harry MacDonnell to have a motive.'

'Why do you think she was so surprised by that?' said Sidney.

'Who knows how that woman's brain works. I still can't get over her thanking us.'

Sidney yawned and stretched his arms. 'I'm hungry.'

'It's only been two hours since breakfast.'

'Well, it's at least time we had coffee.'

'And what do we do about DI Kelso? Don't you want to see what she's going to do?'

Sidney checked his watch. 'It's been forty minutes since she encouraged us to leave. She is obviously in no hurry to go anywhere.'

Ursula sighed and shook her head.

'No point in staying around here,' said Sidney. 'We can stop for coffee on the way home.'

'Right, fine, we'll go for coffee, but don't shout at me if we miss something.' She started the engine and drove away.

* * *

They headed south from Coleraine but within a few miles made a detour to Ballymoney town centre. After parking in Church Street, Sidney was soon enjoying a coffee served with a healthy slice of apple pie and fresh cream. Ursula could only marvel at her father's appetite. She had little enthusiasm for her cappuccino and certainly couldn't eat. They had put the Causeway coast and their investigation behind them, but something still niggled her about DI Kelso's reaction to learning that Teddy and Natalie may have been lovers. The cop had become very distracted and had struggled to continue their conversation. But why? What had she been thinking about? The obvious answer was her sudden need to get to Harry MacDonnell and arrest him on suspicion of murder, but Ursula felt that it was something else. She ran their conversation over in her mind. When exactly had Kelso switched off to her? The detective had repeated her question about the victims being lovers, but was that really the issue that had her dumbstruck?

'Are you enjoying that?' she asked her father.

'It's not bad,' he replied, clearly savouring every mouthful, residual cream on his upper lip.

'Well hurry up, we need to go.'

'What's the rush?'

'Shut up and eat.'

When Sidney had shovelled the last piece of pie into his mouth, Ursula stood up and pulled on her coat. Sidney felt obliged to do the same. His daughter was his lift home.

Seconds after speeding away from the coffee shop, it was clear they were not resuming the southward journey to Holywood. Sidney didn't speak, but merely gazed at Ursula for an explanation.

'Just indulge me for a wee while,' she said. 'I want to check something out.'

The wipers ran at double speed as the van raced towards Bushmills. A short while later, they rolled down the lane and turned into Finn Close.

'I thought we were all done here,' Sidney said with a groan.

Ursula stopped the van in the middle of the close and got out. She stood in the pouring rain, gazing at each of the houses. Sidney had no clue what she was up to, but he needed a little more than her standing there to entice him from the van. Then he watched as Ursula approached number six. Without a car in the driveway, it seemed obvious to him that there would be no one at home. Before Ursula reached the house, the orange door of number five swung open, and Cissy Robinson stepped outside.

'If you're looking for Eleanor,' she called to Ursula, 'she left about twenty minutes ago.'

'Do you know where she was going, Cissy?'

'I have no idea, love, but that policewoman was with her.'

'DI Kelso?'

'Yes indeed. They arrived together in Eleanor's car, stayed about ten minutes then left again. Eleanor had a big bag with her, one of them holdall contraptions with wheels. She didn't look very happy. Come to think of it, DI Kelso didn't look happy either.'

'Thanks, Cissy.' Ursula scurried to the van.

'One other thing,' Cissy called, pointing to Eleanor's house.

Ursula stopped and turned around. 'What's that?'

'Eleanor has left her front door open.'

Chapter 58

Ursula beckoned Sidney from the shelter of the van. Cissy looked on from her front door. Water dripped from Ursula's nose.

'Are you going to tell me what's going on?' He wasn't happy at having to stand in the downpour.

'Ach, Daddy, is it not obvious by now?'

'No, love, you're going have to explain it to your old man. I'm completely lost. What the heck are we doing here, and why is that old busybody watching us?'

'I suddenly realised why DI Kelso was so surprised when we told her that Teddy and Natalie had been lovers,' Ursula quickly explained. 'Then things seemed to get even worse when I told her it was Eleanor who had spied Harry MacDonnell in Finn Close.'

'So? We told her something she didn't know,' said Sidney.

'But then I said that, since they'd grown up together, I had been intending to ask her about Eleanor. That was when she repeated her question about Teddy and Natalie being lovers. She was spooked, or maybe she realised something. I think it was about Eleanor. She remembered something about the woman she grew up with.'

'But what?'

'Well, I don't know. I'm not a genius. But whatever Kelso was thinking, it was enough for her to quickly get rid of us.'

'And you thought it was worth coming back here?'

'Yes, and it seems I was right. Eleanor and Kelso left here together twenty minutes ago.'

'Eleanor has been arrested?'

Ursula wiped the moisture from her face.

'I'm not sure about that, Daddy. I'm thinking that either Eleanor or DI Kelso may be in a spot of bother.'

Sidney opened his phone and called Kelso's number. It went straight to voicemail. Then he tried the number he had for Coleraine police station.

The call didn't take long.

'No one at the station has seen Kelso since lunchtime,' he said. 'What do we do?'

Ursula was already striding towards number six. She called over her shoulder.

'Eleanor left her door open. I'm going for a look inside.'

'Is everything all right, Mr Valentine?' Cissy called.

Sidney grimaced at the sound of the woman's voice. He'd come to hate this place and wasn't keen on any of its residents. He ignored Cissy and hurried after Ursula, who had already entered Eleanor's home.

When Sidney stepped inside, the house was just as he remembered from his first visit. Everything seemed to be in its place. The lounge was tidy. There was nothing to suggest that Eleanor had made a hasty or enforced exit from her home.

'In here,' Ursula called.

Sidney wasn't sure to where 'in here' referred. He went first to the kitchen but found it empty. The next open door was to a rear bedroom. Ursula was staring at a room in disarray.

'What the hell?' Sidney gasped.

'Looks like somebody just had a clear-out,' said Ursula.

A pair of tall antique cabinets with solid doors lined one wall. A smaller sideboard of similar design stood by another. There was no bed in the room, but a wing-backed armchair and an occasional table sat by the window. What begged their attention, however, was scattered over the floor. The cabinets, doors wide open, had been cleared of their contents.

'What is this stuff?' said Ursula.

'I would guess we're looking at treasure.'

Photographs, some in gilt frames, lay on the carpeted floor. Pictures of gold and silver coins, ornate jewellery, weapons, including daggers and swords were interspersed with what appeared to be family photographs. Sidney stooped to pick up a black-and-white picture showing four people in front of a thatched cottage. An adult couple stood behind a young boy and girl of around seven or eight years old. The girl wore an elaborate necklace, presumably made of gold and containing an array of precious stones. Ursula lifted another framed photograph showing only an old man standing by a cottage door. In front of him sat a wooden crate brimming with coins and pieces of jewellery.

'Who are these people?' Ursula asked.

Sidney didn't reply. He was holding several unframed pictures, each showing at least one person displaying items of jewellery and weaponry. Judging by the fading of the prints and by the style of clothing worn, the images were quite old. Sidney guessed at mid-twentieth century. He turned one of the pictures over in his hand.

'Granda Ollie, Lacada Cottage, 20 July 1963,' he read. He examined another. 'Granda Ollie, Granny Sadie, Daddy and Auntie Daisy, Lacada Cottage. Same date,' he said.

Ursula was on her knees, shuffling through the dozens of pictures. She was searching for an image of one person, the woman she believed held all the answers to this mystery. As she examined each picture, she flipped them over in hope of finding a written description. Many of the prints were merely family portraits; an entire history had been dumped on the floor.

Eventually, she turned one over and read the pencilled legend aloud. 'Mummy, Daddy and me, aged 12, Giant's Causeway.' Flipping it over again, she smiled at the image. 'I think this must be Eleanor.' She handed the picture to Sidney and continued sifting through the others.

'Here's one!' she said. She got to her feet and showed it to Sidney. 'Pamela, Teddy and me, June 2001,' she read.

Sidney stared at the colour picture. Teddy McNaughten, a scrawny teenager, stood between Pamela Kelso and Eleanor Martinez, an arm around both girls.

'Are you thinking what I'm thinking?' he said.

'Don't really know what to think.' Ursula sighed. 'We already knew those three grew up together, but why all the pictures of treasure and why these empty cabinets?'

Chapter 59

Cissy had ventured to the front door of Eleanor's house as Sidney and Ursula were about to leave. Sidney held several of the pictures in his hand.

'Is everything all right?' Cissy asked, sounding very concerned. 'I do hope nothing is wrong.'

Neither Sidney nor Ursula was inclined to assuage the woman's fears. If she and others in Finn Close had been truthful from the start, they might not have reached this harrowing situation.

'Are you sure you don't know where Eleanor and DI Kelso were going?' Ursula asked her.

'No. I'm sorry. It all happened so quickly.'

'Check the police station again, Daddy. Maybe Kelso has arrested Eleanor. Cissy, do you know anything about Lacada Cottage?'

'Do you think they might have gone there, love?'

'I don't know. Where is it?' Ursula snapped. This was no time to debate matters.

'It's down a lane near Lacada Point, off Causeway Road,' Cissy said. 'It's not far from our farm, but the cottage is a ruin now. No one lives there.'

'But the place has some connection to Eleanor?'

'Yes, I suppose. It was a long time ago. Eleanor's grandparents lived there, her father and her aunt were raised there. They played with Bertie when they were wee.'

Ursula waited for Sidney to finish his call to the station. He shook his head.

'They've heard nothing from Kelso.'

'Do you think it likely that they've gone to that old cottage?' Ursula asked.

'No real reason to think that except for this photograph,' Sidney replied. He gazed at the picture of a family showing off what appeared to be a hoard of treasure.

Ursula was struck by another possibility.

'Whereabouts did Eleanor grow up?' she asked Cissy.

'Down in Bushmills, round by Primrose Hill. Both of Eleanor's parents are dead; there wouldn't be any family living there now.'

They closed Eleanor's front door behind them and bid Cissy goodbye, requesting that she call them if Eleanor or DI Kelso returned to Finn Close. Soaked from the rain, they hurried to their van.

'I think it's worth taking a look at Lacada Cottage just in case,' said Ursula.

Sidney agreed. 'If those pictures are anything to go by, there is a connection between that cottage, the treasure and Eleanor.'

Three minutes later, they came across a lane they hoped would lead to the abandoned cottage. Sidney, jumping out of the van, found that the metal gate across the entrance was closed but not locked. It was stiff, but he managed to swing it open for Ursula to drive through. Already, it seemed apparent that no one had ventured down this lane for quite some time. Long grass along the centre was undisturbed by feet or by a vehicle. The van lurched from one pothole to another as, at first, they climbed a slight hill then descended on the other side, heading towards cliffs and the sea. Several yards off, they saw little more than a pile of stones. Just one wall with a chimney remained upright of what had been Lacada Cottage. No human had lived there for a very long time.

Ursula managed to turn the van around by driving over a rough patch of grass at the front of the cottage then she attempted some speed back over the hill to the main road. They were running out of options of where to look next for the two women.

'We could try Teddy's cottage,' Sidney suggested.

Back on Causeway Road, they didn't have far to drive to reach the entrance to the former home of Teddy McNaughten. They found it deserted also.

'It's been three quarters of an hour since they left Finn Close,' said Ursula. 'They could be miles away.'

'True, but I wonder if there's something that needs to be accomplished by one or other of those women, like there's unfinished business, if you know what I mean?'

'Daddy, I have no idea what you're on about.'

'Well, let's assume that the treasure in these pictures still exists,' he said, tapping the photos on his lap. 'Assuming also that it had been stored in those cabinets in Eleanor's house, is that what they've taken away in the holdall?'

'So?'

'What are they intending to do with it?'

'Daddy, we're wasting time here. We still don't know whether Eleanor is our killer, and she has been arrested by Kelso, or she's making an escape and taken Kelso with her.' Ursula took a deep breath. 'Or Kelso is the murderer, and she has snatched Eleanor and the treasure. They might even be in it together. Just suggest somewhere else to look next or we may as well go home.'

'Jeez, Ursula, calm down, love. I don't have all the answers, you know.'

'Where to, Daddy?' She tapped her fingers on the steering wheel.

'I have no idea.'

Saying nothing, Ursula suddenly roared away from Teddy's cottage. It seemed to her that the only logical course was to revisit Finn Close. If the two women had not returned, then the police should be alerted, and they could deal with it. As she swung the van into the lane, her path was blocked by a tractor leaving the cul-de-sac and coming towards her. Royston Robinson was behind the wheel. Ursula stopped the van and jumped out. The young farmer opened the window of his cab.

'Hey, Royston, pet, you haven't seen Eleanor Martinez on your travels, have you?'

For a second, she thought the youth had resumed his vow of silence as he wiped his mouth on his sleeve. Life in this part of the world moved slowly, Ursula thought. It moved even slower in Royston's head.

'It's kinda urgent, Royston. Any chance, mate?'

'She passed me on the road a while back,' he said.

'Where, Royston?'

'The main road heading towards Ballintoy.'

'Thanks, pet. Now get out of the way.' She blew him a kiss then rejoined Sidney in the van.

'I know where they'll be,' she said, rolling forward, urging Royston to move back.

When the farmer had reversed down the lane, Ursula turned the van at the entrance to the close then sped away.

'Dare I ask where you're taking me?' Sidney ventured, having detected an increased urgency in his daughter's manner and the van's speed.

'We should have sussed it earlier,' said Ursula. 'She even told us it was her favourite place.'

'I don't recall DI Kelso sharing that kind of personal information with us.'

'Not Kelso; Eleanor! I'll bet she's headed to Carrick-a-Rede, to the rope bridge.'

'Great. Hardly the weather for it.'

Chapter 60

Pulling into the small visitors' car park above the bridge, Ursula saw immediately that her hunch had been right. The only other vehicle in sight was the Toyota belonging to Eleanor Martinez. Hurrying from the van, Ursula quickly checked the hatchback, but there was no one inside. Sidney emerged, struggling to fasten the hood of his anorak in the biting wind. Horizontal rain drove into their faces as they hurried down a winding path towards the rope bridge. This was yet another famous feature of the north Antrim coast, but at that moment, seeing the sights was hardly important to Sidney and Ursula. They both realised it was a matter of life and death and not a place to be in such horrendous weather.

Approaching the steps that descended the cliff to the bridge, they could see two figures on the precarious structure swaying in the gale. On a calm day, the sea in the narrow channel below would be crystal clear, but this afternoon it frothed and crashed in mighty waves against the dark basalt rocks.

Ursula assumed the women were making their way across the bridge to the small island known as Carrick-a-Rede.

Descending the steep steps, Sidney noticed that the women had stopped and were facing each other in the middle of the bridge. DI Kelso was removing things from the holdall and tossing them into the sea. She was first to notice their approach.

'Help me!' Her cries floundered in the gale, but they alerted Eleanor to Sidney and Ursula's arrival.

Sidney took one step onto the bridge's wooden walkway.

Eleanor turned around and yelled at him. 'Don't come any closer!'

She swung a heavy sword towards Kelso, who stood closest to the island.

'Keep going, Pamela,' she shouted. 'Every last piece, one at a time.'

Ursula stepped onto the bridge behind her father. The structure rocked in the wind. The floor comprised of just two parallel planks, the remainder of the structure consisting of stiff ropes and netting. Best not to look down, she thought. The handrails were merely well-tensioned ropes, but Ursula held on tightly, hoping that Sidney was doing the same.

Eleanor, with her back to Ursula and Sidney, supervised Kelso, then briefly, she turned again to face them.

'I said stay back, or so help me, I'll kill her.'

'What's going on, Eleanor?' said Sidney, realising that shouting was the only way to be heard above the roar of wind and sea. He could see that Kelso was greatly distressed, trembling as she threw pieces of jewellery into the sea while trying to remain upright.

'Tell them, Eleanor,' Kelso sobbed. 'Tell them why you're doing this.'

'Shut up, Pamela! If you hadn't been so clever, it would never have come to this. No one else had to die. But you spoiled everything. Just like when we were kids.'

'I didn't do anything, Eleanor. I have never done anything to hurt you.'

'Why are you throwing those things into the sea?' Ursula called.

'She's making me do it,' Kelso replied.

'They mean nothing to me now,' said Eleanor.

Sidney edged closer to the woman.

'Stay back!' Eleanor shouted again. 'Or I swear I'll kill her.'

'You don't mean that, Eleanor,' said Ursula, fighting for her balance. 'DI Kelso is not the person you're angry with. She's only been doing her job. It's all been about you and Teddy, hasn't it?'

'None of your business. You're supposed to be looking for that whore Fiona McCabe.'

'Fiona? What harm has she done to you?'

'She was another of Teddy's women. She is nothing but common trash.'

'But she only worked for Teddy, nothing more,' said Sidney.

Eleanor scoffed.

'She filled Teddy's head with silly notions. I mean, what was she thinking that *my* Teddy would be interested in winning the lottery? He didn't need all that money. Not when he could have me.'

She thrust her hand into a pocket of her raincoat and pulled out a piece of paper.

'And here it is.' She laughed. 'The winning ticket that everyone has been looking for. Teddy waved it in my face on the night I killed him. He told me it was a winning ticket and he and Natalie were rich. He'd gone too far; I couldn't bear the pain any longer. I snatched it from his hand after I stuck a dagger in his heart.'

Still managing to hold the sword, she ripped the paper into several pieces and released them to the wind. No one would ever know if it really was a jackpot-winning ticket.

'He broke my heart, so I broke his.'

'Teddy never loved you, Eleanor,' said Kelso, who had stopped dumping the treasure, although there was little remaining in the holdall.

'Don't you dare say that,' Eleanor screamed. 'Teddy told me that he loved me, and I loved him.'

'But Eleanor, you were only fifteen years old, what did any of us know at that age?'

Eleanor pointed the sword at the policewoman's throat.

'No, Eleanor!' Ursula shouted.

'Teddy loved me first before he ever went near you, Pamela,' Eleanor cried.

'I know,' said Kelso weakly, 'but you must also know that I never encouraged him. He asked me out once, but I turned him down. I never loved Teddy.'

'If you loved Teddy so much, why did you kill him?' Ursula asked.

Eleanor swung around, swiping with the sword.

'Because he didn't love me back,' she said. 'When he moved into that cottage at the Causeway, he became obsessed with *Girona* treasure. This rubbish.' She indicated the gold and jewels now despatched to the ocean. Snatching the bag from Kelso, she threw it into the sea. 'I moved to Finn Close just to be near him. I hoped that one day he would want me again. But he never did.'

In floods of tears, Eleanor hacked at the ropes with the sword. Fortunately, the blade of the ancient weapon was entirely blunt. Given time, she would probably succeed in cutting through, but Sidney wasn't prepared to wait. He launched himself at the strong woman. The sword fell from her grasp, slipped through the netting and disappeared in the turbulent sea. Eleanor dropped to the floor with Sidney on top of her.

'No! Please!' Eleanor cried. 'Let me die here.'

'Not today,' said Sidney.

Kelso and Ursula rushed to his aid. The three of them hauled Eleanor to her feet and carefully led her off the bridge. As they climbed the steps to reach the path, Eleanor proceeded to recount more of her story. She was already calmer now, although the venom hadn't left her voice. She seemed eager to impart her truth, relieving herself of a story she had suppressed for years. Ursula and Kelso held her by the arms; she didn't seem capable of walking unaided, her knees buckling beneath her. Sidney massaged his back. He'd had too much excitement for one day.

Chapter 61

'When my granda passed away,' Eleanor sobbed, as they trudged up the cliff path, 'I had no close relatives left. Mummy and Daddy were already gone and Aunt Daisy too. I had always known about the treasure that Granda had locked in a big trunk in his bedroom. He had kept it his entire life. His grandfather had found it behind a wall in an old barn near Dunluce in the 1880s and realised what it was straight away. The story in the family was that he had intended to sell it and use the money to buy his farm. But then his wife died in childbirth at the age of twenty, leaving him heartbroken. He locked the treasure away at Lacada Cottage and never spoke of it again. My granda simply kept it out of respect for his own grandfather. When the family were all gone, and there was no one left at Lacada, I brought the trunk to my home. I locked the treasure in a cabinet, hidden away just as my granda had done.'

Sidney listened to the history-teacher-cum-murderer with interest but wished she'd save her story until they reached the shelter of the police station or even their vehicles. But the woman continued to pour out her family history, her voice strong enough to be heard above the noise of the wind and sea.

'Each time I met Teddy, which wasn't often because I now realise that he avoided me whenever he could, he always prattled on about how he was close to finding a hoard of treasure from the *Girona*. If only he knew, I used to think, but I never said anything. A few months ago, I met him one morning on the Causeway, and as usual he was rabbiting on about searching for treasure. He said he was amazed that I, as a history teacher, wasn't showing much interest in his quest. I couldn't help myself. I just snapped. I told him that I loved him, had always loved him, and yet he wasn't loving me back. He just laughed. Told me to grow up. As he walked away, I finally told him about the treasure. Of course, he didn't believe a word I said. He told me I was pathetic. I swore to him that I was telling the truth. He came right up to me and laughed in my face. I was in tears. He tramped all over my feelings.'

Eleanor stumbled, but Ursula and Kelso prevented her falling. The only strength the woman possessed now was reserved for telling her story.

'You don't have to explain this now, Eleanor,' said an emotional Kelso. 'Wait until we get to the station.'

'But I want to, Pamela. I have to say it here. This was our happy place.'

They carried on, Eleanor still supported by Ursula and Kelso.

'One day when I knew Teddy was out on one of his tours, I left some pieces of my treasure in a bag at his front door. I didn't leave a note of explanation or even my name. I hoped he would guess who had done it. That night he called me. He didn't even have the good manners to come and see me face to face. He was only interested in knowing where I'd got the stuff and how much more I had. I refused to tell him, so he lectured me about keeping it hidden away. He told me that I should hand it over to the authorities, insisting that none of it was mine to keep. I told him I wasn't interested in the treasure; I only wanted him and I to be together just like when we were kids. Then he seemed to doubt I was telling the truth. His final words were to tell me that even if I had the treasure, he would never want it because it came from me. He would never love me, not for all the treasure in the world. A few days later, I was standing on Carrick-a-Rede, at the very spot where he'd kissed me for the first time when we were fifteen and told me that he loved me. I decided then that I would put him out of his misery.'

'But why kill Natalie?' Ursula asked, struggling to hold back her own tears at the tragedy unfolding.

They'd reached the car park. DI Kelso had called for backup and, while they waited, Eleanor launched into a further tirade in answer to Ursula's question.

'That woman was a slut. Divorced, you know. She'd discarded her husband and there she was moving into my street and fornicating with my Teddy. You should have seen her, dressed in those degrading clothes. And she had Teddy dressing up too. Disgusting. I shed no tears when I saw her trying to get away that night. She'd found Teddy dead yet only thought of herself. I took a sword from Granda's treasure and caught her before she could drive out of the close. I had intended that she would get the blame for killing Teddy then die on the Causeway like it was suicide. But when we reached the shore, she became hysterical, tried to fight back, so I ran her through with the sword and pushed her off the rocks. She meant nothing to me.'

Chapter 62

Feeling stiff and sore from his recent exertions, Sidney made the most of his last breakfast at the Armada. They'd decided on another night in Bushmills rather than driving home through the storm they'd battled at Carrick-a-Rede. His enjoyment of a full Ulster fry was soon diminished, however, by a visit from his favourite north Antrim police detective. She did at least accept the invitation to join them, although she restricted herself to a coffee.

'Eleanor will be charged later today,' she said.

Ursula detected the sadness in DI Kelso's tone. She looked weary; her eyes were tired and puffy, her face pale. Ursula wouldn't be surprised to hear that she hadn't slept.

Sidney nodded, said nothing and continued eating.

'I suppose I should thank you,' Kelso continued. 'If you hadn't turned up yesterday, there would have been two more bodies. After speaking with you at the station, I went to the school to question Eleanor, but she was desperate to show me the treasure. It was my mistake; I should have arrested her and brought her to the station, but for some reason I still couldn't believe she was a murderer. When we got to Finn Close, she opened her cabinets and showed me everything. Then she turned on me and put a sword to my throat.'

'Do you really think Eleanor would have killed you?' Ursula asked.

'I believe so; there was no way she was going to give herself up. Yesterday, when you told me that Teddy and Natalie had been lovers, I realised that Eleanor would not have been happy witnessing that situation. I'd always known that she carried a torch for Teddy, but I never imagined she'd ever do anything about it. I certainly didn't believe her capable of murder. She always lived in hope that one day Teddy would come for her. Such a shame. She could have met someone else and been perfectly happy.'

'So, Teddy and you were never a couple?' said Ursula.

'Ooh no. Two reasons for that. Firstly, I never fancied him in the slightest and secondly, even if I had, I would never have hurt Eleanor like that. I suppose when Teddy died, I didn't want to believe that Eleanor was involved. It was easier to suspect others, especially when you pair were running around looking for Fiona McCabe.'

'What about all that treasure you threw in the sea?' said Ursula.

'We'll wait for a calm day and send in a boat and some divers. Whatever we find will probably go to the museum.'

'It's amazing that it was kept secret within one family for so long,' said Sidney.

'Eleanor never breathed a word of it,' Kelso replied. 'To her the treasure was only of sentimental value. It was her family heirloom.'

The detective sipped her coffee and, sounding brighter, changed the subject.

'What about your case of the missing Fiona?'

Sidney explained about the lottery syndicate and the infighting that ensued when they believed they'd won.

'Whether they'd won or not, Eleanor put an end to it when she ripped up that ticket,' he said. 'I've never come across such a band of untrustworthy people before.'

'If you wish to bring charges against them for holding you captive, Ursula, you have my support,' said Kelso.

'Thank you, but I think it's best forgotten. Besides, I'm quite fond of big Royston now.'

The cop's eyes widened, and from somewhere within she summoned a smile.

'I'd best be getting to work,' she said. 'It may be the weekend, but I have to take a formal statement from Eleanor.' She rose from the table and suddenly that sarcastic gaze reappeared. She looked at Sidney who was chewing on a piece of rather stubborn bacon.

'Promise me one thing, Mr Valentine.'

'What's that, DI Kelso?'

'You'll think twice before taking another case up here. Please, go home to Belfast and stay out of trouble.'

'Holywood,' said Sidney.

'Whatever.'

Chapter 63

Ursula had the rear door of the van open wide and was packing the equipment required for a day of surveying potholes. Sidney was looking forward to it.

'It's therapeutic,' he'd claimed during breakfast. 'None of that frantic running around on the north coast.'

Ursula smiled, knowing it wouldn't be long before either of them wished they had another interesting case on their hands.

This morning was bright and calm, if a tad cool, but in this part of the world you can't have it all, not at the same time. Ursula waited by the van. She was ready to go, but Sidney was supposed to be clearing up in the kitchen. Suddenly, she was aware of someone behind her.

* * *

'Daddy, look who I found,' she said, coming into the flat.

Sidney looked up from his recliner; he'd managed to sneak in another coffee before Ursula came looking for him. A woman stood next to her with a thin smile and big eyes behind enormous glasses.

'Hello, Mr Valentine,' she said.

'Which one are you?' was all that Sidney could manage.

'It's Eve, Daddy,' said Ursula as if it were obvious. 'Have a seat, Eve. I'll get us some coffee, since my father isn't making the effort.'

'I thought I should come to thank you and pay what I might still owe,' Eve said, choosing a stool at the breakfast bar, perhaps feeling more at ease closer to Ursula than Sidney. 'And to apologise for the trouble I caused you.'

'No further charge,' said Sidney. 'In the end the murders weren't connected to your hiring us.'

'I know, but I put you both in danger over something that now seems so selfish and silly.'

'Have you been in contact with Fiona?' Ursula asked.

'She called me to apologise. She's asked if she can come home to Eden.'

'How do you feel about that?' said Sidney.

'How can I turn my sister away? Eden is our family home. She's not comfortable living back at Finn Close, not after everything that's happened with her neighbours.'

'I can imagine,' said Ursula with a chuckle. 'Any news of the lottery win?'

The woman shuffled a little and adjusted her glasses.

'I'm sorry that it was the real reason behind my hiring you. I thought that if I sent you up there asking after Fiona, you would eventually stumble on the winning ticket or at least identify who had it. But while there was a chance, I had to get my hands on that ticket before Fiona. Unlike her, I would have shared the money with the others in the syndicate. Teddy should never have been trusted to place the entry for that week. And he could have prevented all that trouble if only he'd checked the results and told everyone.'

'Seems rather unimportant now since the man lost his life,' said Ursula. She glimpsed her father who appeared to have dozed off in his recliner. She knew he was thinking.

'What did Fiona say about it?' he mumbled. 'Did she reckon it was the winning ticket?'

'Oh yes, she's certain of it. According to her, the winning line of numbers was the one she used every week as her personal entry. The win would have been hers and not the syndicate, but no one was ever going to believe her.'

'And the winning ticket was the one Eleanor ripped up and threw in the sea?' said Ursula.

'It seems so,' said Eve with a sigh, 'unless someone else has it.'

Eve dabbed her eyes with a tissue, then rose to leave.

'Thank you so much for all that you did,' she said.

'You're welcome, Eve, or should I call you Fiona?' said Sidney.

'Behave, Daddy,' Ursula scolded.

'Well, you can't believe what anyone tells you these days,' said Sidney. 'I've never seen the two of you together.'

'I'm sorry, Mr Valentine. I really am Eve, and I live in the Garden of Eden.'

'If you say so, love,' Sidney replied. 'Watch out for the snakes.'

'Teddy and Natalie might not have died if we hadn't been so obsessed about a winning lottery ticket,' Eve said.

'I wouldn't blame yourself,' said Ursula. 'A woman like Eleanor, totally obsessed with a man who didn't love her, was always going to find an excuse to end her pain. The murders were about unrequited love and jealousy, not about a winning lottery ticket.'

'What will you do now?' Sidney asked.

'Fiona and I jointly own our late parents' house in Eden. We'll live there until we can sell it. I'll split the money with Fiona then make a fresh start somewhere else.'

Eve McCabe walked away. Ursula closed the door behind her.

Chapter 64

Eugene hurried through his morning postal round in Bushmills. He had parcel deliveries to do later at Portballintrae, but he had more important business to conduct before then. It was a bright morning, and the sun shone in his eyes as he strolled along Main Street popping letters through the doors of houses and delivering bundles to various shops. When he reached the Spar, he went inside and handed a pile of mail to Myrtle, the owner. She was another friendly gossip of the town and the main source of news. Cissy Robinson was part of her social network.

'How's it going, Eugene love?' she asked.

'Not too bad, Myrtle.'

'I'm sure you're relieved all that nasty business is out of the way.'

'I am indeed.'

Eugene produced a slip of paper from his pocket and handed it to the shopkeeper.

'I think it's a winning ticket, Myrtle,' he said failing to hide the excitement in his voice. 'Would you check it for me?'

'Aye, certainly.'

The sixty-year-old woman smiled as she fed the ticket into the lottery machine while Eugene looked on.

'Boyso! Congratulations, Eugene!' she cheered. 'You've won!'

Eugene threw his arms in the air.

'Yes!' he yelled.

'Now don't go spending it all on the demon drink, young man. It'll do you no good.'

'Thanks, Myrtle. I won't.'

Eugene had scarcely bounced from the shop before Myrtle had lifted her phone and called her friend.

'Hello, Cissy. I've just had young Eugene in the shop. You'll never guess. He's only after winning a tenner on this week's lottery.'

* * *

A crisp wind blew from the sea, rustling the long grass. A big tractor sat by the gate, its driver on foot meandering back and forth, a solitary figure on a speculative mission. He'd traversed half the field, the dairy herd looking on with little interest. It required patience, but he had all the time in the world to spare. Isolated in his world of hope, all he had to do was listen. He'd already clocked up several false dawns, but it had not deterred him. Suddenly, as he swept his arm to the right avoiding a fresh cow pat, he heard a beep. He hovered over the spot and his machine delivered further beeps to his headphones. Sweeping in an arc with the device, the beeping intensity rocketed. It was going daft. He pulled off the headphones.

Royston laid Teddy McNaughten's metal detector on the ground, said nothing, lifted his spade and began to dig.

List of characters

Sidney Valentine – private detective
Ursula Valentine – Sidney's daughter and private detective
Eve McCabe – Sidney and Ursula's client
DI Pamela Kelso – Coleraine police detective

The residents of Finn Close

Cissy & Bertie – retired couple
Eugene – postman
Eleanor Martinez – history teacher
Curtis & Julie – young couple
Fiona McCabe – Eve's sister
Natalie MacDonnell – young divorcee

Other characters

Teddy McNaughten – tour guide at Giant's Causeway
Gary – Teddy's employee
Karen – barmaid at the Armada Hotel
Walter Robinson – farmer
Royston – Walter Robinson's son
Martin Dawson – police constable
Dr Arleen MacIntosh – archaeologist

If you enjoyed this book, please let others know by leaving a quick review on Amazon. Also, if you spot anything untoward in the paperback, get in touch. We strive for the best quality and appreciate reader feedback.

editor@thebookfolks.com

www.thebookfolks.com

Also in this series

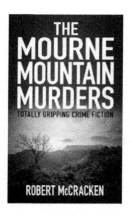

THE MOURNE MOUNTAIN MURDERS
(Book 1)

Father and daughter Sidney and Ursula make an unusual private detective team. But hitherto they've survived the tough streets of Belfast. Yet when curiosity gets the better of them and they probe into a murder, they'll attract the unwanted attention of a nasty criminal gang. Can they outwit the mob, or are their days numbered?

FREE with Kindle Unlimited and available in paperback.

More books by Robert McCracken

THE DETECTIVE INSPECTOR
TARA GROGAN SERIES

Merseyside Police detective Tara Grogan scarcely looks
old enough to be a police officer never mind a detective
inspector. Maybe because of this she is more
determined than most to prove herself capable when
investigating murder on the streets of Liverpool. But
her tendency to become emotionally involved in cases
frequently places her in great danger and undermines
her efforts to get on in the force.

FREE with Kindle Unlimited and available in paperback.

BOUND TO RUN

A romantic getaway in a remote Lake District cottage turns into a desperate fight for survival for Alex Chase. If she can get away from her pursuer, and that's a big if, she'll be able to concentrate on the burning question in her mind: how to get revenge.

FREE with Kindle Unlimited and available in paperback.

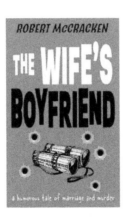

THE WIFE'S BOYFRIEND

Charlie Geddis is thrown out by his wife but, determined to win her back, decides to prove that her new boyfriend, a property developer with a lot of assets, is in fact a lying crook. In the process, he becomes embroiled in a web of bribes, infidelities and possibly a murder.

FREE with Kindle Unlimited and available in paperback.

Other titles of interest

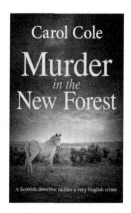

MURDER IN THE NEW FOREST by Carol Cole

When a woman's body is found on the ground next to her horse, it seems an unfortunate accident had occurred. However, DI Callum MacLean, newly arrived in the picturesque New Forest from Glasgow, suspects differently. But hunting a killer in this close-knit community, suspicious of outsiders, will be tough. Especially when not everyone in his team is on side.

FREE with Kindle Unlimited and available in paperback.

THAT CARE FORGOT by James Warren

Junior attorney Rebecca Holt isn't too happy when given the pro bono case of a convicted murderer. Yet Nick Malone isn't really interested in his parole hearing, rather he is obsessed with a serial killer who terrorized New Orleans in the 1990s. When Malone reveals his secrets, Rebecca is faced with a life-changing decision.

FREE with Kindle Unlimited and available in paperback.

As a thank-you to our readers, we regularly run free book promotions and discounted deals for a limited time. To hear about these and about new fiction releases, just sign up to our newsletter.

www.thebookfolks.com

Printed in Great Britain
by Amazon